THAT'S LIFE, SAMARA BROOKS

THAT'S LIFE, SAMARA BROOKS

Daniel Ehrenhaft

DELACORTE PRESS

All rights reserved. Published in the United States by Delacorte Press, an imprint of Random House Children's Books, a division of Random House, Inc., New York.

Delacorte Press is a registered trademark and the colophon is a trademark of Random House, Inc.

Visit us on the Web! www.randomhouse.com/kids

Educators and librarians, for a variety of teaching tools, visit us at www.randomhouse.com/teachers

Library of Congress Cataloging-in-Publication Data
Ehrenhaft, Daniel.
That's life, Samara Brooks / Daniel Ehrenhaft.—1st ed.
p. cm.
Summary: When thirteen-year-old Samara devises a genetics experiment to cover up her involvement in a middle school gambling scheme, she and two classmates make a discovery that causes them to question their beliefs about God, aliens, or "Whoever-you-Are."
ISBN 978-0-385-73434-9 (hardcover) — ISBN 978-0-385-90441-4 (lib. bdg.) — ISBN 978-0-375-89595-1 (e-book)
[1. Gambling—Fiction. 2. Genetics—Fiction. 3. Faith—Fiction. 4. Adoption—Fiction. 5. Middle schools—Fiction. 6. Schools—Fiction. 7. Family life—Fiction.] I. Title. II. Title: That is life, Samara Brooks.
PZ7.E3235Thd 2010
[Fic]—dc22
2009005013 .

Book design by Marci Senders

Printed in the United States of America

10 9 8 7 6 5 4 3 2 1

First Edition

FOR THE D.G. NEPHEW POSSE:
Kirk V, Henry, Ethan, and caleb

First and foremost, I'd like to thank Wendy Loggia—for both her tireless patience and her vision in seeing this book through. I'd also like to thank all the rest of the good folks at Delacorte Press, especially Beverly Horowitz, Krista Vitola, and Kathy Dunn. Props are also due to my wonderful agents, Edward Necarsulmer IV and Sarah Burnes, and to the generous readers who helped along the way with their invaluable insight, particularly David Levithan and Leslie Margolis. A big thanks to Ricardo Cortes, as well, for his awesome illustrations. And as always—last but never, ever least—a shout out to my lovely wife, Jessica, for her sharp eyes.

God does not play dice
with the universe.
—Albert Einstein

Actually, I'm pretty sure God
does play dice. God just bets a
little differently than we do.
—Samara Brooks

The Prelude,
the Finale, and
the Secret Inside the
Buried Thermos

To whom it may concern—

To someone who might stumble upon this thermos and open it by pure chance—

To the three of us ten years from now—

To our families, to the grown-ups we know, and to planet Earth in general—

We're 99% sure we're doing the right thing by burying this tonight. From what we've seen, the world isn't ready for it. Or maybe it isn't ready for the world. Or maybe both.

For starters, it proves something that nobody was supposed to know—something that is still blowing our minds (Samara's mind most of all) and will in all likelihood continue to blow our minds until we are old and wrinkled and gray.

On top of that, it might also possibly prove something huge and unfathomable (Nathan's words), something that has never been proven before—and that, if true, would change all of human history and the way we look at the universe, forever. Which is a lot to handle.

So: We solemnly swear to keep the contents of this thermos a secret. It will remain our secret until we return to this spot to dig it up exactly ten years from today. We're hoping we'll be able to make more sense of it when we're grown up. And since grown-ups don't make a lot of sense, we also know we're taking a big gamble. But we'll worry about all that in ten years. At the very least we hope we'll be able to figure out how to break the news to everyone.

Finally, we wish we had something better than an old thermos to bury it in. But when it's late at night and you're stuck out in the middle of the woods and all you want to do is go home and take a bath, you get kind of desperate. So we apologize to our future selves and whoever else if it smells like rotten chicken soup, or worse.

SWORN TO SECRECY:
Samara Brooks, Lily Frederick,
and Nathan Weiss

3

Part One
Samara Brooks

Our Common Language

Before I get beyond the basic stuff you need to know about me—my name (Samara Brooks), my age (thirteen), my hair (black), my weight (forget it), that heinous mole next to my nose—there is one thing I'd like you to know about a certain theory of the universe. The theory goes: If humans ever come into contact with an alien intelligence, our common language will be math.

Say a UFO lands and a strange creature walks out. Odds are that we won't be able to welcome it with a big "Hi!" The creature might not even speak. It might just snort, or gesture with whatever limbs it may have, or try to beam its thoughts telepathically. So we will have to find a way to break the ice. And almost every Nobel Prize–winning scientist out there believes that math is the only natural extraterrestrial icebreaker. In short: Once we figure out a way to count to five with, say, a fire-breathing land squid, pleasant chitchat is sure to follow. *"Sweetie, I'm so glad you visited Earth. And that outfit is so cute on you. It matches your tentacles!"*

I mention this because math is also the common language of con artists.

God

Just so you know, I will be conning you for the remainder of this story. I think it's only fair that I tell you up front. On the other hand, I will also be completely honest. That may sound like a contradiction, but it isn't. I will be conning you in the sense that I'll try to get you to see things from my point of view, so I might leave out certain vital information that would allow you to see things differently.

In other words, I won't *lie*. I just might not tell the *whole* truth.

Here's an example: I've already left out some vital information. When I was speaking about an alien intelligence, I was also speaking about God.

You know who else leaves out certain vital information, other than con artists?

God.

Okay, I realize that some people might be offended that I call God an "alien intelligence." Some people might also be offended that I decided to run a gambling ring out of my school's cafeteria at the beginning of eighth grade, and that I nearly swindled my class president out of sixty-three bucks. If you fall into either of these categories, please put this book down and go buy *Chicken Soup for the Soul* or some such and live happily ever after. But if you enjoy a good con, stick around.

An Outstanding Balance of $441.50

It's hard to pinpoint the exact moment when the insanity began, but I figure it's probably best to start with my first big creative writing assignment of eighth grade. As scribbled on the board by my English teacher, Mr. James, it read: *Make me laugh! Describe the funniest moment of your summer vacation!* ☺!

THE FUNNIEST MOMENT OF
MY SUMMER VACATION
BY SAMARA BROOKS

My summer vacation didn't have any funny moments. Seriously, I'm trying to think of one. It wasn't tragic or anything, but "funny" isn't a word that leaps to mind. We didn't go on any funny trips to funny places. We didn't go anywhere, so really, it was more of a summer break than an actual vacation. Plus, my parents were both super-busy. My dad's trying to make partner at his law firm, so he works insane hours. My mom works at a nonprofit organization that tries to help poor people. This is a good and noble cause, of course, but she had to stay late almost every night of the week. Maybe there were more poor people than usual. Sorry if that sounds harsh.

Anyway, I know I'm supposed to make you laugh, but I only laughed—like really, truly "Ha-ha-ha!" out loud—just once. It was at dinner last week, when I swindled my brother, Jim, out of five dollars.

Picture the dinnertime scene: Jim and I were home alone, eating macaroni and cheese in the living room. I was trying to watch *Celebrity Poker Showdown*. Jim, as usual, was staring into a massive math textbook with a look of panic on his face. His big nose started twitching, the way it always does when he's freaked out.

Jim's nose looks like a beak. Not that this really means anything, but still, I mention his beaklike nose because at times like these, I feel like writing BIRDBRAIN on his forehead. Jim is about to be a senior and he can barely add two and two. Worse, he's applying to MIT and plans to take AP Calculus this fall. He wants to be a big-shot scientist.

"Just help me with this statistics problem," he begged.

"Not now," I told him. "Come on, I'm watching

this. It's the final round. I'll bet you anything that fat guy from *Law and Order* will fold."

"Samara, if you don't turn off the TV, I'll fart. I mean it."

I hit the mute button. "Jim, your statistics problem isn't the problem in front of you. Your statistics problem is that you don't *understand* statistics. So here's my help. Statistically speaking, chances are about one in eight billion that you'll get into MIT. So just watch this round with me."

"What kind of seventh grader even talks like you? You're like Dr. Frankenstein."

"Technically I'm an eighth grader now."

"Whatever. If you don't help me, I'll tell Mom and Dad that you lied about giving up Blackjack.com, and you'll be in big trouble," he said. "I bet they'll take your laptop away."

Since I'm a gambler by nature, I knew that Jim had the upper hand here. I hadn't given up Blackjack.com. Hardly. I'd been spending at least three hours a day on it, if not more. But what else was I supposed to do? I'm too young to get a job, and my parents didn't want to pay for another year of camp. Best just to quit while I was ahead.

"Fine, I'll help you," I told him. "But I'm upping my fee to five bucks per equation."

"Deal," he agreed.

Ever since I was ten and Jim was fourteen, I've been helping him with his math homework. First algebra, then trigonometry, and now this. He made me swear never to tell Mom and Dad because he doesn't want them to find out that he isn't really the brilliant mathematical genius he claims to be. I'm hoping they'll figure that out for themselves, but who knows?

My starting price when this whole shady deal began was a dollar per equation. Now we were at $4.50 per equation, and that was for an "open-book" final exam, so the answers were right in front of him. Not that I've had much luck collecting. Jim prefers to write me IOUs. In fact, I've only collected $13.50 of fees totaling $455.00.

"You're really willing to pay me five bucks for a statistics problem?" I asked.

"Yeah, but here's the thing," he said, as usual. "I don't have the five bucks on me right now. I spent it on this delicious feast we're eating. Somebody's got to feed us, right? I can hardly even tell if Mom and Dad live here anymore. So here's what: I'll write you an IOU. When Mom and Dad show up, I'll get some money from them and pay you. Deal?"

Jim grinned at me like a con artist. That's when I laughed.

THE END

PS: Mr. James, just a suggestion, but wouldn't it be more fun to write a creative essay about a billion-dollar caper or a seedy political cover-up or a spy adventure or something?

The Key to Storytelling, care of Shakespeare

Mr. James asked to see me after class the next day. It was only the second day of school. I wasn't off to a great start.

"Is this essay true?" Mr. James asked once the other kids had filed into the hall.

"Word for word," I said. "That's why I included the quotes."

He paused for a moment. "Do you know Shakespeare, Samara?"

"Not personally."

Mr. James pursed his lips. "Yes. Well, I mention Shakespeare because we'll be reading some of his plays this year. And when we do, I'd like you to think about something. I'd like you to think about how Shakespeare *shows* rather than *tells*. I'd also like you to think about that in terms of your own writing."

"You'd like me to think about writing like Shakespeare?" I asked.

"Yes—I mean, no, not exactly." He sighed. "Samara, I know you're very good at math. And people with good math brains tend to prefer having things spelled out in a by-the-numbers way. Sometimes they may even have a hard time appreciating the things that *aren't* spelled out for them. But Shakespeare won't tell you, 'Hamlet is a troubled soul.' Instead, he'll *show* you Hamlet's inner torment. Does that make sense?"

I shrugged. "I'm not really sure," I said. "I haven't read *Hamlet* yet."

"You'll see what I mean when you do," he replied. "And I'd like you to try rewriting your essay afterward, with an eye toward showing, not telling."

"Okeydokey," I said.

I still haven't read *Hamlet,* but I'll bet Mr. James is probably right. Telling is a lot easier than showing. So now I'm going to tell you about Mr. James: He's bald, and his tweed jacket sometimes smells like overripe fruit, and he claims to have written a novel called *Auburn Autumn*—but if he did, it must have stunk, because I can't find it either on Amazon.com or in the bookstore. Plus, he uses words like "inner torment" in regular conversation, and I'm pretty sure he isn't a huge fan of people with good math brains.

In this same spirit, I am going to tell you why I decided to run the gambling ring out of my school's cafeteria. That way, I won't have to waste your time trying to "show" you why—whatever that even means—and we can get straight to the action.

Oh, and you can forget about Mr. James for now. He doesn't become important again until a little later on.

Exacerbating circumstances

Odds are that I wouldn't have even started gambling at school if it weren't for one important detail I left out of my back-to-school essay. My summer vacation had a major *un-*funny moment right at the end—the night of my thirteenth birthday.

Not so coincidentally, this was also the night before school started. I say "not so coincidentally" because my birthday is September 4. Given that school always starts the Tuesday after Labor Day, chances are one in six that my birthday will fall that very same night. These are pretty good odds if you're a gambler, but lousy odds if you're hoping your birthday will be barrels of fun, even without what my dad calls "exacerbating circumstances." (He uses this term a lot in his job.) In non-lawyer-speak, exacerbating circumstances are various little things that make a crappy situation even worse.

Take my twelfth birthday. That was the night my parents told me I was adopted.

In some ways, I shouldn't have been that surprised. For one thing, I already knew Jim was adopted. As a matter of fact, Mom and Dad had told him the night of *his* twelfth birthday. (They'd even picked the same place: Mozelli's Pizza Palace.) But still, it didn't go over very well. Not that I burst into tears or anything, but I just didn't understand why they'd waited until now to break the news. Couldn't they have told me when they told Jim? To make matters worse, they wouldn't tell me who my real parents are.

Whether they knew and didn't want to tell me, or whether they didn't know themselves, they wouldn't say. They still won't.

What they *would* say was that the news didn't change anything. I was still their daughter. They were still my mom and dad. Just not biologically.

As it turned out, they were wrong. Not about our biological relationship, of course, but the news did change something: the way I looked at life. If I wasn't Mom and Dad's biological daughter, then I wasn't really Samara Brooks—at least, not the Samara Brooks I'd thought I was. So really, I could be anyone I wanted to be.

It was an *opportunity*. As such, I should make the most of it.

That's why I'd decided to sign up for Blackjack.com that fall—and also why I'd signed up multiple times, under multiple identities. You're not supposed to gamble online unless you're over eighteen, but if you're making yourself up as you go along, age doesn't really matter. That's the beauty of Blackjack.com. *Everyone* makes themselves up. And everyone's anonymous. The happy result: Everyone fits in.

The reason I mention all this?

"Fitting in" turned out to be the big topic of conversation exactly one year later: the night of my thirteenth birthday.

Grown Up Beyond My Years

So there we all were, back at Mozelli's Pizza Palace, huddled over two large sausage and mushroom pies. I'd just dug into my second slice. The restaurant was noisy, tinkling with silverware and buzzing with conversation—or maybe it just seemed that way because nobody at our table was talking. Nobody was even really eating, except me. Mom and Dad kept looking at each other. Jim kept looking at them, then at me, then back at his plate. Dad kept scratching his chin, too, which is what he tends to do when he's about to apologize or deliver some unpleasant news.

"What's going on?" I finally asked.

Dad pushed his untouched pizza aside. "Samara, your mother and I would like to discuss something with you." He lowered his voice. "Something important."

My stomach lurched. For an awful moment, I thought they were going to tell me that they were getting a divorce. Given what they'd sprung on me last year, any bombshell was possible.

"We know you can handle it, because you've always been mature beyond your years," Mom added. "It's one of the things we love most about you."

"You aren't getting a divorce, are you?" I asked point-blank.

Dad's face softened. "Of course not. Your mother and I are as committed to each other and to our family as we've ever been. It's why we both work so hard."

He didn't sound like himself. He sounded as if he were reading lines from a bad TV script. All of a sudden I wasn't hungry anymore, either. "So what's the matter?"

"Nothing," Mom said. "It's just that . . . well, we'd love to see you make a few changes this year. It's your last year at Madison Middle School."

I leaned back in my chair, nervous. "What sorts of changes?"

"We'd love to see you make an effort to, well, fit in," Dad

said. "And I know that's a silly term, and I feel bad even using it because you *are* so grown-up . . ."

His voice faded as if a giant volume knob had been turned down. I wasn't sure how I was supposed to react. I thought about how Jim had reacted when my parents put *him* on the spot about "making changes." He usually kept quiet in a situation like that.

My eyes darted to Jim. He shrugged and flashed a grin as if to say, *I've been there.* Then he took a huge bite of sausage and mushroom pizza.

I glanced at my own plate.

Looking back now, I remember thinking: *Jim has the right idea.* Best just to eat and let my parents ramble. It was still my thirteenth birthday, even without the exacerbating circumstances. I might as well make the most of it before the pizza got cold.

Drama

Back home that night, lying in bed and staring at the ceiling, I didn't think about the changes I would try to make—or even where I was supposed to start.

Mostly I thought about the first day of school, and how every year there were always a few kids who came back after having completely reinvented themselves.

Last September, Constantine Romulus waltzed into seventh grade with a Mohawk and a tattered leather jacket painted with the words PUNK ROCK!!—prompting nonstop whispers and giggles until October. Wendy Melvin, once shy and mousy, reappeared with painted nails and her blond curls ironed straight, made up like a scandalous teen celebrity. Jim told me that she was secretly dating a freshman at Madison High, some guy named Moe—a rumor I still haven't fully confirmed.

Maybe it was *my* turn to reinvent myself. Which begged two questions. Who would I be? (No offense, but I couldn't picture myself with straight blond hair or a Mohawk. Anyway, Constantine Romulus had since had the sense to return to a normal hairdo.) And . . . would anybody even notice?

I wasn't exactly big on the Madison Middle School radar to begin with, which was the whole point. In fact, I was practically invisible. Not that I fell into the angry loner category (at least, I hoped not), but certain social lives do require a major time commitment: phone calls, texts, IMs, sleepovers, makeovers, public fights, public make-ups . . . in a word, drama. The kind of drama that people like, say, Wendy Melvin lived for. Even Jim lived for drama, which was probably what kept him from learning the basics of math. Then again, I'd never been included in any drama, good *or* bad.

For some kids, Madison Middle School was the center of the universe. For me, ever since I'd started in the sixth grade—and last year in particular—it was just a place to show up on weekdays. I'd never wanted or needed it to be anything more. I had *Celebrity Poker Showdown*; I had Blackjack.com . . . I even had Jim in his spare time, if I was desperate for company, which I hardly ever was.

I could hear him next door, giggling into the phone. "No, dude, that wasn't Kristen's underwear, I swear. . . ." The rest was muffled, except for a loud "Ha!"

At that moment, as I lay stretched out on my back, a thought occurred to me. Jim might have stunk at math, but he'd figured out something that I never quite could, even after two whole years at the same school: how to break the ice with other people and create some drama. To my credit, I suppose I'd figured out something *he* hadn't: how to gamble and con people using math—and specifically, statistics.

I wondered if there was a way to combine the two.

The old Samara Brooks probably wouldn't have made the effort. The old Samara Brooks probably would have grabbed some headphones to drown out Jim, then logged on to Blackjack.com and spent the rest of the night playing with the same old crew of anonymous gamblers out there.

But that wasn't me anymore. If I was really going to make

some changes for Mom and Dad's benefit, then I was through being anonymous.

Before I could think twice, I rolled out of bed, hopped over to my desk, and popped open my laptop. In less than two minutes, I banged out an announcement, care of the new, unanonymous Samara Brooks. I took a deep breath and smiled, then pressed print. I pressed it again, and again . . . ten times in all: ten copies to hang in strategic locations around Madison Middle School first thing tomorrow morning.

WELCOME BACK STUDENTS!!!
EVER PLAY BLACKJACK?
EVER PLAY CRAPS?
FEEL LIKE GETTING LUCKY? FEEL LIKE BEING A WINNER?
FEEL LIKE MAKING $$$?
THEN MEET *ME*, SAMARA BROOKS, AT LUNCH PERIOD TODAY!
I WILL BE AT THE TABLE NEAREST THE CAFETERIA EXIT,
READY TO PLAY!

The Insanity Begins

The signs didn't last long.

Somebody at school—probably a teacher like Mr. James, possibly Mr. James himself—tore them all down before the end of second period.

By lunchtime I wondered if anybody would even remember them. Maybe putting myself on the Madison Middle School radar would be more difficult than I thought. Which wasn't the biggest tragedy in the world, I supposed. But as soon as I sat down, Lily Frederick, our eighth-grade class president, strolled right up to my table. She welcomed me with a big "Hi!"—as if I were an alien emerging from a UFO.

"Hi!" I said back.

Lily Frederick makes a big effort to be nice to everyone all the time, which is probably why she wins elections so easily. She's constantly in motion, hopping from one person or group to the next. Maybe it's her toothy smile or her perfectly even pigtails, but she's always struck me as the kind of person who thinks that a camera could suddenly appear out of nowhere and snap a photo—so she'd better be prepared.

Needless to say, we don't have a whole lot in common. Well, except for our noses. They're both small, with moles nearby. Hers is just a tiny bit more crooked than mine.

I don't know why I'm so fascinated with noses. I think it's because everyone's nose is different, but nobody ever mentions how or why. On detective shows, the cops always talk about fingerprints or voice matches or DNA, but never noses. Have you ever seen somebody with the exact same nose as you, though? Point being: Con artists like to think about things that nobody ever talks about. It helps give us an edge.

"Samara, I saw your signs, and I think it's such a great idea," Lily said. "I've always wanted more excitement in the cafeteria, you know? Something to make lunch more than just a meal? And see, gambling is something I've always wanted to try. My parents are totally huge fans of Vegas, and I've always wanted to go. But the thing is, whenever my parents go for a weekend, they make me stay with my aunt Esther. She doesn't really like Vegas, you know? I mean, Aunt Esther takes me to church a lot, which is fine because I like church. But that's another story." When she finished, she laughed.

I wasn't sure what to make of all that. "Well, I'm glad you think it's a good idea," I told her. "This isn't Vegas. But hopefully it'll be lots of fun. Lunch *should* be more than just dry hamburgers and runny Jell-O, don't you think?"

Lily laughed again. "Yes!" She pulled out a chair and sat across from me.

"So, you really want to give gambling a shot?" I asked.

"I really do," she said.

"Okeydokey." I dug into my backpack for a deck of cards.

A couple other kids turned, watching us from afar. I kept a wary eye out for any teachers. But if our class president approved, I figured there wouldn't be much of a problem—

not unless she was setting me up. I highly doubted Lily Frederick was the type, though, unless *she* had reinvented herself over the summer. Besides, *I* was the con artist. For the first time all day, I felt pretty decent.

"Do you know how to play blackjack?" I asked.

"Yeah, I think so. You get dealt two cards, and you try to get your cards to add up to twenty-one, right? And you can't go over. So maybe you bet on a third card?"

"Exactly," I said. I wasn't telling the whole truth, though. She was right about all the card stuff, which is just the math part of blackjack. No card has a higher value than eleven. Kings, queens, and jacks—"face cards"—equal ten. Aces can equal either eleven or one: your choice, depending on what you need to get to twenty-one. But the fun part of blackjack, the part she didn't mention, is trying to beat the dealer. That's where the drama comes in. Up to eight can play, which means seven different people can try to beat the dealer at once. But since we were alone, we were looking at a two-person game. Statistically, two-person games are the easiest for the dealer to win.

"A dollar per hand, okay?" I said. "Whoever loses has to pay up."

Lily nodded. "No problem."

I split the deck and shuffled the cards with a quiet

machine-gun clatter, and then dealt two apiece—both of hers faceup, one of mine facedown.

Lily studied the cards: the eight of clubs and the eight of hearts. I held the king of diamonds and a mystery card. That made ten points so far . . . ten to her sixteen.

"Hit me," she said. She flashed a nervous grin. "Is that the right thing to say?"

"Mm-hmm." I dealt her a third card, facedown. She would probably lose if I didn't draw another card. (Statistically, she had a less-than-seventeen percent chance of winning.) But when we showed each other our hands, it turned out I'd dealt her the four of spades—so her hand added up to twenty. I held a king and the nine of clubs: nineteen.

Her eyes lit up. "I won!" she exclaimed as if she'd just struck gold.

I smiled, digging into my pocket and fishing out a dollar bill. I wasn't upset about losing. Not in the least. What Lily didn't know was that I'd chosen the two most addictive games when it comes to gambling: blackjack and craps. Neither is complicated, and they both move fast—which means that once you learn the rules, you generally tend to keep betting and betting.

"How about we play again?" I suggested.

"Definitely!" she said.

As I shuffled the deck, a little crowd of spectators began to form. I dealt Lily a seven and an eight: fifteen. By sheer coincidence, I dealt myself a jack and an ace: blackjack.

The crowd oohed.

"Oh well," Lily murmured, deflated. "One more game?"

The cards were already in motion. "Why stop at one?" I said.

Lily lost the next round, too: nineteen to seventeen. And the round after that: eighteen to fifteen.

By the time the bell rang, she'd lost fourteen straight and owed me twelve dollars.

"Samara, I'm really sorry," Lily said sheepishly. Her eyes darted to the clock on the cafeteria wall. "I only have five dollars. Is it okay if I pay you the rest tomorrow?"

"No problem," I told her. "You can even hold on to the five and pay me the whole amount tomorrow if you want." I didn't want her to feel embarrassed. Besides, in the grand scheme of the universe, twelve bucks wasn't all that much. Jim owed me $441.50. I'd even been in the hole myself once or twice on Blackjack.com, which was why Mom and Dad didn't want me to spend any more time on it.

Not that I needed to share any of that with Lily. I figured there was just the right amount of drama between us for now.

Luck, and Why It Stinks

Understanding coincidence is a big part of gambling. If you can see coincidence for what it is (nothing more than a freak occurrence given a certain set of statistical probabilities), then you're in good shape. But if you believe that coincidence has some sort of higher meaning, that it is proof of something beyond math—of something divine or alien, of something *meant* to be—you'd probably end up owing me money, too.

This was something Lily Frederick could never quite figure out. Then again, most people can't, which was why I had a hunch my gambling ring would be a success.

As a con artist, you offer people a thrilling bet, like trying to befriend somebody, or picking the right card—or even proving that aliens, in fact, do exist. And you use that risk to your advantage because you know a big secret about statistics that a lot of people don't: Most thrilling bets are bound to be losers. But the fact is that most of us believe we'll win, especially if we get lucky just once.

Nathan Weiss's Statistics

Lily wasn't the only one waiting for me at the lunch table the next day. A half dozen other kids wanted to gamble, too, including Wendy Melvin, Constantine Romulus, and Nathan Weiss. I mention Nathan Weiss specifically because if there's anybody more invisible than me at Madison Middle School, it's him—although, of course, being "more invisible" is by definition impossible. His vital statistics:

• He always wears corduroys and button-down shirts, even when it's hot.

• If he combed his hair right, his messy brown bowl cut could possibly look like a scruffy rock star's instead of a dork's. (I don't think he owns a hairbrush.)

• He spends all his time in the library and the science lab because he's obsessed with UFOs and mysterious "codes." This makes him nearly impossible to understand, although weirdly fascinating to listen to.

• Like me, he's also very good at statistics. Not *these* sorts of statistics, but the kind that deals in probabilities, the kind Jim stinks at—and the most crucial kind of math for con artists, since it helps us predict how certain bets will turn out.

Lily's Debt Adds Up

Lily smiled apologetically as I sat down at the table. "Hey, Samara? Listen, I'm really sorry, but I forgot to bring the twelve dollars," she said.

"That's okay," I said. "Maybe I'll end up owing *you* twelve dollars."

She blushed. "You think?"

"Anything's possible," I said—though, to be fair, I was conning her. I glanced at the crowd, pulled the pack of cards out of my knapsack, and split the deck. "Who's in?"

Wendy, Constantine, Nathan, and three other kids I barely knew—probably because they weren't in any advanced math classes—jostled for chairs.

I shuffled and reshuffled. The cards flew around the circle in a merry-go-round whirl, and then came loaded silence as eight pairs of eyes examined eight pairs of cards.

I held a ten of spades and nine of hearts. There were four calls of "Hit me," three calls of "I'll stand." I dealt four more cards, faceup . . . and bingo: That left me the winner. Everyone else held hands of either over twenty-one or under eighteen.

Everyone wanted to play again, too—most of all Lily.

The cards flew around the table once more. And once more after that.

By the time the bell rang, Lily Frederick had racked up a total debt of twenty-one dollars.

Not Interested in Interest

"Samara, I'm really, really sorry," Lily moaned. "I don't have a penny on me."

"No problem," I told her again. I wasn't worried. Besides, she wasn't the only one who owed me now. Wendy Melvin owed me eight dollars, Constantine Romulus owed me six, and Nathan Weiss owed me nine—just to name a few.

Coincidentally, none of them had any money on them, either.

Wendy Melvin was the first at the table to offer an excuse. "Samara, here's the deal: My boyfriend borrowed all my cash this morning." She even went so far as to show me her empty wallet, tapping a painted fingernail on the leather. "But I swear you'll get your money soon . . . *with interest.*"

Constantine's excuse was a lot more creative. "Samara, my family spent the summer in Moscow, and we still haven't changed any of our rubles back to dollars." He rumpled his spiky hair. "As soon as we do, I'll get you the money . . . *with interest.*"

The best excuse, however, belonged to Nathan Weiss—and he wasn't even trying to con me. "Samara, I know this will sound nuts, but I swear I think I'm on the verge of cracking a medieval code that will prove aliens exist. And once I do, I bet money won't be a problem anymore. Then I can pay you back . . . *with interest.*"

The funny thing was, I hadn't mentioned interest. I didn't care about interest, or even really about making money. Still, as a con artist, I had to pretend I cared; otherwise, nobody would take me seriously.

"Just bring what you owe me tomorrow," I called after them as they scurried off to class. I had a feeling they wouldn't.

counting to five

Back home that afternoon, I realized I'd made a big dumb mistake. I'd started a gambling ring without asking anybody to buy chips first.

At every single casino on the planet, even the casinos online, you have to buy chips before you start playing. That way, the money part is taken care of up front. If I'd brought chips to school that first day—and made sure that everybody who wanted to gamble bought a minimum of, say, ten dollars' worth—then nobody would be in the hole right now. Lily probably wouldn't have even wanted to play. Now that it occurred to me, a lot of other people wouldn't have wanted to play, either.

Whatever. People were playing *now,* so I decided to make a new rule: Starting tomorrow, anybody who wanted to play blackjack at lunch would have to buy a minimum of ten dollars' worth of chips. Plus, the people who already owed me wouldn't be allowed to gamble anymore until they'd paid me. (To be fair, I wouldn't charge interest.) I started rummaging through my closet, searching for the poker set Mom and Dad had given me for my tenth birthday.

There was a knock on my door. "Samara?" Mom asked.

"Yeah?"

She poked her head inside. "I was able to get off early from work for once! I wanted to see if you—" She spotted me in front of the closet on all fours, tossing some stuffed animals aside. "Is everything okay?"

I nodded, wondering if she and Dad had stowed the poker set in the basement without telling me. They'd done that before with birthday presents they'd given me and then sort of wished they hadn't, like my chemistry set, which was great for creating homemade stink bombs and not much else.

"Yeah. I'm just trying to find . . ." I paused. If she knew that I was looking for poker chips, then she would ask why. I didn't exactly feel like telling her that I'd set up a casino at school. "I was trying to find my chemistry set," I finished.

Mom tapped her chin. "You know, I think I remember seeing it in the basement. Jim might have borrowed it and then forgot to put it back."

"Oh yeah. That sounds right." I sat on my bed.

"Planning a major scientific experiment?" she quipped.

"Well, I *was,* but then I remembered that there's no point trying to outdo the Madison Middle School science department anymore," I replied dryly. "Not with its fabulous electron microscope."

32

Mom giggled.

The Madison Middle School's electron microscope had become something of an inside joke around our house, ever since it had been donated to the science department last year. There'd been a lot of hoopla surrounding it, because apparently no other middle school *owned* an electron microscope. The punch line was that no one knew how to use it. Whenever I complained about having too much English homework or something, Jim would say, "Everybody should be as lucky as you, Samara. Do you know how many kids would kill to go to a school with a *fabulous electron microscope*?" Then Mom and Dad would pretend to agree (if they were around), and we'd all laugh and repeat the words *fabulous electron microscope* over and over a zillion times.

Come to think of it, it's one of those had-to-be-there inside jokes that probably isn't so funny to anyone else.

"Maybe when Jim's a famous scientist, he'll return to Madison Middle School and show everyone how to use its fabulous electron microscope," Mom said.

I laughed. "Anything's possible."

"And who's to say *you* won't be a famous scientist?" Mom suggested. She beamed at me. "Math skills definitely run in the Brooks family."

"I'd put my money on Jim becoming a famous scientist before me," I said. "The fame thing is way more up his alley."

Mom glanced down the hallway toward Jim's room, and then poked her head in farther. "Samara, I'll bet you didn't know this," she said quietly, "but Jim didn't become Mr. Popular until he started high school. He sometimes had a hard time fitting in during middle school, too."

I tried not to laugh again. If she was trying to make me feel better, she should have tried a different strategy. Jim had *never* had a problem fitting in. If anything, he'd fit in too well. He'd been the only eighth grader ever to be voted both Class Clown *and* Most Likely to Succeed.

"Mom, did Jim ever ask you who his real parents are?" I heard myself ask. I wasn't even sure how the question had popped out. I wished it hadn't.

"We're his real parents, Samara," Mom said gently.

"I know. I'm sorry. I just—"

"No, no, you don't have to apologize," she said. "He never asked us who his biological parents are. But he did have lots of questions. He never hesitated to ask them, either. You know you can ask us anything, right?"

I nodded. I had a very good feeling that Jim *had* asked who his biological parents were—just not in front of me. But I decided not to call Mom on it.

"Well, I'm going to go make dinner," she said finally. "I think we're going to barbecue tonight. Feel like helping with the grill?"

"Um . . . maybe in a little bit?"

"Sure. I'll leave you to your big scientific experiment." She smiled again and closed the door.

I sat there for a while. I completely forgot about the poker chips. I never did remember to find them.

It's funny, though. If you start with the lie I told Mom about looking for the chemistry set, and include the lie Mom told me about why it was in the basement, then throw in the lie I told her about giving up on a big scientific experiment, and finish with the two lies Mom told me about Jim . . . that adds up to a total of five different lies Mom and I told each other in an effort to communicate.

We'd managed to count to five together. I figure that's a nice accomplishment, even though neither of us is a fire-breathing land squid.

Sixty-three Dollars in the Hole

Lily bumped into me in the hall the next day after second period. Her face was droopy, as if she hadn't slept so well. There were purple rings under her eyes. Even her freckles seemed paler than usual.

"Whew, Samara, there you are!" she exclaimed. "I've been looking for you."

"What's up?" I said. "Are you all right?"

"Oh, yeah!" She laughed and twirled a pigtail, nervously glancing at the passersby. "I mean, sure, I'm fine. I was wondering, though, would there be any way for us to sneak in a round of blackjack before lunch? You know, just you and me?"

"To tell you the truth, I was thinking about skipping blackjack today," I said. "I was supposed to bring these poker chips for people to buy, but I forgot."

"Please?" She stifled a yawn.

I peered at her suspiciously. "Are you sure you're okay?"

She nodded several times. "Yeah. I'm sorry. See, I was up late, doing some research on blackjack, and I wanted to see if what I learned actually works in a real game. If we play, it can totally count, like we're playing at lunch. We'll gamble for money."

The bell rang. The crowd in the hall began to dwindle. "Won't you be late for class?" I asked. "I have third period free, but . . ."

"It's just English," Lily said dismissively. "Mr. James won't mind."

"Are you sure? Whenever I'm late, he makes a big deal of marking it down."

"Please, Samara?" She dug into her skirt pocket and handed me a deck of black cards with frilly gold lettering that said *Viva Las Vegas!* "Listen, we can play right here." She scooted over to a water fountain and sat cross-legged on the floor beside it, slapping the tile. "One quick round. For all the money I owe you."

I sat down across from her. "All right," I said, reluctantly shuffling the flimsy deck. The cards nearly popped out of my fingers. "But just this one round." For some reason I felt nervous, even though she was the one making a twenty-one-dollar bet.

I reshuffled, then dealt her a six of hearts and six of diamonds faceup on the floor between us. Then I dealt myself a card facedown, followed by a ten of spades.

"Is it okay if I split my hand?" she asked carefully.

"Um, sure." *Wow.* She *had* been doing some research. If a player gets dealt two of the same card, like Lily had—a six of hearts and a six of diamonds—the player can split the hand and start over with both. In other words, she could play two hands against me at the same time. The more hands in play, the less likely the dealer will win.

I dealt her a nine of diamonds for one hand, and a six of spades for the other.

Lily twirled a pigtail, and then pointed at the nine of

diamonds. "I'll stay there." She tapped the six of spades. "Hit me here."

Chances were that I wouldn't deal a card that put her over twenty-one. (Given all the probabilities of what cards remained in the deck—plus given the cards I held in *my* hand, the ten and the queen of hearts—those chances were less than sixty-seven percent, though at the time neither of us knew what I held. We only knew of the ten. Of course, given my cards, chances were more than ninety-two percent that she'd lose anyway. It's true. You can do the math.) I figured if I lost, Lily would be happy enough to quit—hopefully for good. Owing me money was clearly stressing her out. It was starting to stress *me* out.

"Hit me," she repeated. "And I want to double down."

I couldn't believe it. Lily Frederick had used blackjack lingo twice in one sitting. It didn't sound very natural, though, which I didn't take as a very good sign. She sounded as if she were trying to speak a foreign language. "Are you sure that's so smart?" I asked. Doubling down meant that if she lost, she'd owe me three times as much as when we'd started: sixty-three dollars. She'd owe forty-two dollars for that game, plus the twenty-one she already owed.

Lily nodded. Her eyes remained pinned to the cards. "I'm sure. Hit me again."

The bell rang a second time. Third period had begun. Lily and I were the only ones left in the hall. I took a deep breath and pulled out a card.

By the luck of the draw, it was the king of clubs. That put her at twenty-two.

Her eyes widened. She gaped at me, and then down at her freak occurrence of a losing hand—and without a word, she hopped up and bolted.

I Won't Break Your Legs
or Anything

Lily never showed up at the cafeteria for lunch that day.

I went ahead and told the other usual gamblers that blackjack was off until I brought chips to school. Nathan Weiss did manage to finagle three games of craps out of me, though. He lost all of them, putting his total debt at twelve bucks. Mostly I played on the condition he wouldn't talk about aliens. I guess I wasn't in the mood.

When I finally tracked down Lily in the hall near the gym, right before fifth period, her hair was around her shoulders. I wondered if she was trying to disguise herself. As soon as we spotted each other, she unfolded a huge algebra textbook in front of her face—upside down. She quickly right-sided it, but not before our eyes met again.

Oh boy. I trudged over and tapped her on the shoulder. "Um, Lily?" I said. "I have your cards. Do you want them back?"

Her shoulders sagged. The book fell to her side. "You can keep them," she moaned. "Samara, I'm so sorry. I really thought I could win with one big bet."

"It's okay, Lily. Just pay me whenever you can."

"Well, that's the thing." She raised her eyes. "See, I owe you so much now that I'll have to ask my parents for the money. Which means I'll be in big trouble. They don't want me to gamble. It's, like, the only rule they've ever given me. Even though *they* go to Vegas. They don't even go to church. *I'm* the one who goes to church. You know? But if they ever found out I owed you sixty-three bucks . . ." She didn't finish.

I nodded. Even though I didn't relate to the church part, I could definitely relate to the not-wanting-to-tell-your-parents part.

"It's not that big a deal at all, Lily," I reassured her. "Take as long as you want to pay me. I won't break your legs or anything."

Big Mistake

For a long time, Lily and I just stared at each other. Then she started to giggle. So did I. It was a pretty ridiculous thing to say. Once we started, we couldn't stop.

Suddenly she raised a finger to her lips. "Shhh!" Her head jerked toward a closed door a few feet down the hall.

I knew the door well. It's thick and forbidding, and it's always closed. I imagine there's a door like it at every school, the one marked TEACHERS' LOUNGE.

"I thought I heard your name," she whispered.

The voice behind it was muffled, but we both recognized it: It belonged to Principal Horowitz.

We tiptoed closer.

"It's not Lily Frederick's fault, Henry," he was saying. "It's my fault. It's this betting nonsense in the lunchroom. I should have put an end to it the first day of school."

Lily's eyes widened. So did mine. Talk about coincidence. Principal Horowitz happened to be complaining about *us*.

"All this money changing hands can't be a good thing," another voice said.

Hmm. The other voice belonged to Mr. James. Who knew his first name was Henry? Henry James, the English teacher. It made sense, in a coincidental way.

"I have to tell you, I felt bad about having to mark Lily absent today," Mr. James added. "It's the first time she's ever cut class. She probably wondered if her presidency was in danger. She looked as if she was about to faint."

Lily frowned at me. "Not true," she mouthed silently.

Principal Horowitz started to chuckle.

"What's funny?" Mr. James asked him.

"Oh, nothing." He sighed. "I was looking at my lesson plan for American history. Next week we'll be studying Richard Nixon. He always ends up being one of the students' favorite bad guys. And I was thinking about what John Dean said." His voice rose in mock seriousness. "'A cancer is growing on this presidency!'"

"And that cancer is Samara Brooks!" Mr. James added in the same silly tone.

The two of them cracked up, sounding a lot like my family did when we made fun of Madison Middle School's fabulous electron microscope.

At that moment, I did something I shouldn't have. I started giggling again, too—much louder than before.

Lily shook her head and slapped my arm. I would have done the same thing in her shoes.

Sure enough, the door flew open, and Principal Horowitz stepped outside.

what I Didn't Spell out for Lily

In my defense, I had two good reasons for giggling.

The first was that I recognized that John Dean quote, too—so, like Mr. James, I got Principal Horowitz's joke. The quote is pretty famous, at least if you're into history or famous con artists, or both. (I make it my business to learn all about history's failed con artists so I won't make the same mistakes they did.) John Dean was a lawyer who worked for Richard Nixon, who, in addition to being a failed con artist, was the thirty-seventh president of the United States. John Dean grew so sick and tired of all of Richard Nixon's conning that he told him right to his face, "A cancer is growing on this presidency!"

The second reason I laughed, which is probably just as complicated:

In spite of various noble efforts, nobody has found a cure for *real* cancer. Still, we keep on trying. Likewise, we keep on playing our hands at a million other lofty bets, which I think is kind of tragic because most lofty bets are doomed . . . but also sort of beautiful, too, because it shows that most human beings like to gamble in a way that might matter. Yet all the while, everybody at Madison Middle School—grown-ups and students alike—keeps gambling on getting the best of each other.

Not that there was much point in trying to explain all that to Lily.

A Funny Lie About Fear

"Excuse me, but what's going on here?" Principal Horowitz asked. He sounded more embarrassed than annoyed.

"I was just asking Samara for some help with my algebra homework," Lily said. She held up the textbook. "I was having some trouble with a word problem."

Principal Horowitz turned to me. "Is this true, Samara?"

"Yes," I lied. "Lily stinks at word problems."

In truth, Lily is and always has been a very good math student. She's in almost as many advanced math classes as I am.

Principal Horowitz twisted his lips and adjusted his tie. "That's not a very nice thing to say about Lily," he said.

"But it's true," Lily protested. "I *do* stink at word problems."

"So this has nothing to do with these card games at lunch?" he asked.

I turned to Lily. She could have very easily answered yes. She could have said that it *did* have to do with the card games at lunch, and that I'd pretty much suckered her into owing me a lot more money then she could handle. But she didn't. I didn't speak up, either. And in that brief instant—sharing a small silent lie with Lily Frederick, with Principal Horowitz looming over us—I thought: *We've managed to count to one together, Lily and I.* For the first time all day, I felt decent. Go figure.

Lily shifted on her feet. "Um . . . can I go now? I've got class."

"Yes, of course," Principal Horowitz groaned.

Lily's eyes fell, and then she scrambled off, her hair swishing behind her back. I still wanted to return her cards, but that would have been an even dumber move than laughing right outside the teacher's lounge. It probably would have seemed weird to Principal Horowitz, too.

Mr. James stepped out into the hall. His eyes narrowed until they turned into slits no thicker than a folded hand. Then he hurried in the opposite direction.

"Out of curiosity, Samara, how much of our conversation did you overhear?" Principal Horowitz asked uncomfortably.

"Don't worry," I told him. "I'm pretty sure you don't *really* think I'm a cancer growing on Lily Frederick's presidency."

"Yes. Well. You're right, of course. And I apologize. People sometimes take things out of context, you know." He cleared his throat. "In any event, I suppose it is lucky I bumped into you. I'm afraid I'm going to have to call your parents about the card games. Betting isn't allowed, Samara."

I giggled one last time. I couldn't help it.

"Did I say something funny?" he asked.

"Not really. It's just that you said *you're* afraid of having to call my parents. I'm the one who should be afraid, right?"

The Inspiring Photo on Principal Horowitz's Wall

I'd been to Principal Horowitz's office once or twice during my years at Madison Middle School, but this was my first eighth-grade visit.

He'd redecorated a little. Not for the better, no offense. The sun-filled room had lost its homey feel. Maybe he wanted it to seem more grown-up or something. The fish tank was gone, and so were all the plants and the corkboard photomontage of his wife. The only picture left on the wall was a framed photograph of him in the science lab, standing next to the electron microscope's old-fashioned computer console. In it he was grinning and giving a thumbs-up.

Principal Horowitz paced back and forth. He pressed the phone tightly against his cheek in a vain attempt to call my dad.

"I don't think you'll reach him," I offered in the interest of saving time. "He's really busy. He's trying to make partner at his law firm."

Principal Horowitz raised a finger to his lips.

"I don't think you'll reach my mom, either," I whispered. "She's been working, like, twelve-hour days trying to help the poor."

The bell rang. I was late for English, not that I minded. I

slouched down in the chair across from Principal Horowitz's desk. After another minute, he sat down and hung up the phone.

"I can't even get your father's voice mail," he said. "It's full."

"Welcome to my world. My brother isn't even sure if our dad still exists."

He sighed. "I have to be honest, Samara. I've known you for two years, and I still find it hard to understand you sometimes."

I opened my mouth, and then hesitated. For some reason, I'd started to fixate on that photograph on the wall, right behind him. The words *fabulous electron microscope* echoed through my head . . . and with them the image of my mom, standing in my bedroom doorway last night. *"Planning a major scientific experiment?"*

"It's funny you say that," I said slowly. "Because I want to propose something."

He almost smiled. "I'm not sure if that's wise."

"Don't you want to hear me out? What do you have to lose?" I should have kept my mouth shut, but at that point I figured I didn't have much to lose, either.

"I think you should just get to your next class," he said. "In the meantime, I'll keep trying to reach your parents."

"Just give me two seconds," I pleaded. "I know you think Lily Frederick is a good person. And she *is*. But so am I. Well, maybe I'm not as good as Lily. But we're the same. You see where I'm going with this?"

Principal Horowitz arched an eyebrow. "Not really."

I leaned forward. "Let me explain. Lily is different from me in certain ways. But we're still the same because we're human. We even have the same noses. Well, almost. So how about if I prove that scientifically? Not the noses part . . . What I mean is, if you're going to call my parents, you should call hers, too. She gambles at my table during lunch because she *wants* to. But that doesn't make her a bad person. Any more than that makes *me* a *good* person. We're all human beings. We're all made of the exact same stuff."

"Samara, you just admitted that you're not as good a person as she is!" He took a deep breath. "Sorry. I should really discuss all this with your parents."

Should you, though? I wondered. Yes, staring at that photo on his wall, a complex con had taken shape, and there was no slowing the momentum. It was a con that revolved around math and science . . . and more specifically, using math and science in a real live experiment—and best of all, one that I could even explain truthfully to my mom if I had to. Which was why the ridiculous-sounding words that

48

tumbled out of my mouth were "Principal Horowitz, what do you say we finally figure out how to use our fabulous electron microscope?"

The Story Behind the Fabulous Electron Microscope

Before we get to Principal Horowitz's answer—

I should tell you a little more about the microscope. I'm one of the few kids at school who know the whole scoop.

First off: Electron microscopes are hard to come by. The cheapest used one sells on the Internet for around eighty-five thousand dollars. Plus, they require expert care and massive amounts of electricity. They use tiny subatomic particles to form images on computer screens. Normal microscopes, on the other hand, use light to form images through glass lenses.

To put it another way, the microscopes in *your* science lab can probably magnify something by up to two hundred times. They make small things look bigger. Our crappy, clunky, thirty-year-old electron microscope, even at its worst, can magnify something up to five hundred thousand times. You can use it to observe the tiniest particles in existence, the atoms that make up everything in the universe.

Needless to say, nobody has ever been allowed to touch it except Principal Horowitz and our science teacher, Mrs. Belle.

Here's how they got their hands on it.

In the early 1970s—right around the time John Dean yelled at Richard Nixon—a scientist at our local university bought the microscope with a huge grant he received. His name was Dr. Chance.

A few months later, the university fired Dr. Chance for raising a big fuss about a guest lecturer who was coming to speak, a preacher named Dr. Willis.

Dr. Willis believed, and still believes, that God created Earth about six thousand years ago. This would mean that nothing on Earth is older than that: not dinosaur bones, not the oceans or mountains, not even the rest of the universe. He also believes that anybody who disagrees with him will spend eternity in a lake of fire. You might have seen him on TV. He always wears flashy double-breasted suits.

Dr. Chance called Dr. Willis a dirty name (I can't print it here)—and screamed that Dr. Willis wasn't even a real doctor, and that people like him had no business coming to a university in the first place to corrupt young people with lies. But Dr. Willis went ahead and made his speech anyway. He also called Dr. Chance a heathen and promised to donate to the university ten times what Dr. Chance received with his grant.

The money must have made the people in charge of the university extremely happy, because they kicked Dr. Chance off the campus the very next day. And even though the electron microscope weighed close to a ton—and came in several complex segments (screen, generator, console, plus a bunch of cables and wires)—he single-handedly loaded it up into a truck and drove it away. It belonged to him, after all.

Not long afterward, another university offered him a job. Their science lab had an even *better* electron microscope. So he donated his old one to the Madison Police Department—on two conditions. He told the police to use it "to study the *real* crime scenes, like the local university" and "to put away the *real* crooks, like Dr. Willis." Those were his exact words. They were even printed in the *Madison Tribune*.

The problem was, nobody knew *how* to use it.

So it sat in the basement for the next thirty-seven years or so until a forensic scientist moved to Madison to work for the police department. His name was Dr. Belle.

He didn't know how to use it, either.

But his wife happened to be a scientist, too, and she took a job teaching science at Madison Middle School. The two of them thought that a big electron microscope was a neat thing for the school to have, and that Mrs. Belle could figure out how to use it in her spare time. Plus, the police department would get a huge tax rebate if they donated the microscope to the school for charitable purposes. The police could then use that money to purchase forensic gadgets that they could, in fact, use.

And that's pretty much it.

With the help of several police officers, Dr. and Mrs. Belle loaded up the microscope into a truck and drove it to Madison Middle School, where it sat in the science lab unused because Mrs. Belle had a lot less spare time than she'd thought she would have. And there it remained until the day after I came up with my con.

Principal Horowitz's Response and the Aftermath

"What does our electron microscope have to do with anything?" Principal Horowitz asked tiredly.

"Well, you know how everyone has unique fingerprints or noses, but we're all still the same?" I asked.

"I suppose so," he said.

"Well, how about if we use the microscope to examine my DNA and Lily's DNA?" I asked. "Mrs. Belle can supervise, and we'll break the old thing in—long overdue anyway. I can *prove* to you that Lily and I are the same. I'll draft a hypothesis tonight that you and Mrs. Belle can review. It'll be a genuine scientific experiment. Just give me tonight; that's all I need. And if you think it's bogus, you can call my parents. I'll even make sure they're around."

"A genuine experiment, eh?" he mused.

"You can even suspend me or something if you find out I'm pulling your leg."

He leaned back in his chair and chewed the tip of a pen. "I probably shouldn't agree to this. But seeing as I shouldn't keep you here any longer, and you're late for class, and your parents are unreachable anyway . . . you're on."

"Really?" I was a little surprised. Maybe he still felt bad for calling me a cancer on Lily Frederick's presidency, even if it was a joke.

"Yes. We *should* figure out how to use the microscope," he said. "It certainly takes up enough space in the lab. But you better have this hypothesis of yours to me first thing in the morning."

"You got it," I said. "I'll e-mail it to you before school."

He almost smiled again. "Okay, Samara," he said. "Good luck."

I heaved a sigh of relief. That was easy. All I had to do was stay up late tonight and write a little paper, something I'd already done this week. And the coolest part was that if we *did* figure out how to use the microscope, everyone would be able to examine the stuff that made up both Lily Frederick and me at the tiniest microscopic level.

Maybe I'd even prove Mom right after all. Maybe I *would* become a famous scientist. At the very least, I had an idea that would show everyone that the structure of Lily's DNA and my DNA were exactly the same.

What I didn't know was that I had just conned myself.

Part Two
Nathan Weiss

BEFORE WE GET to what happened next, I want to state for the record: Yes, I do believe in aliens. And yes, I believe that God is an alien, too. That's right, the same God I learned about in Hebrew school—the one who parted the Red Sea and gave Moses the Ten Commandments, and who thinks everyone should rest up one day a week because he took a day off, too.

Why do I believe this? Well, that's a whole other story. But if you're curious, I'd recommend reading anything by Erich von Däniken.[1] Seriously. It'll blow your mind. I should warn you, though, some of it is hard to understand. But so is a lot of stuff—like why a card shark would suddenly cancel black-jack on you because she decided to make up a new "money-for-chips" rule.

It didn't really make much sense. I was already twelve bucks in the hole.

Anyway, I wanted to put my views on God right up front, like Samara did, because our very first fight ever was about—you guessed it—God.

The trouble started that Friday.

---

[1] He's the author of a book called *Chariots of the Gods.* It's a huge bestseller from the 1970s that tries to prove aliens visited Earth in UFOs thousands of years ago, and that ancient human beings mistook them for gods, or even *the* God. (With a capital *G.*) Google it.

I arrived at school early, as usual, around seven-thirty a.m. Classes start at eight. Call me a geek (you won't be the first), but I like to use the library when it's empty. That way, nobody can peek over my shoulder and rag on me for what I'm reading. Our science teacher, Mrs. Belle, likes to get to school early, too, so she always lets me in. Normally, it's just the two of us, but today Principal Horowitz had beaten us both. He sat alone at the long table in the middle of the room, right in front of the checkout desk, squinting at some papers.

I cleared my throat. "Hello? Principal Horowitz?"

He glanced up and smiled. "Nathan, there you are. I've been waiting for you."

"You have? Why? Am I in trouble?"

He laughed. "Not that I know of. Should you be?"

"No," I said. "I just like to use the library early."

"So I've heard. I don't mean to alarm you, Nathan." He waved a hand at an empty chair directly across from him. "No reason to be jumpy, I promise. Mrs. Belle told me I might be able to find you here."

I crept forward and sat down.

"Nathan, I've noticed that you've been spending lots of time with Samara Brooks and the others at the cafeteria this week, playing card games," he said. "So I wondered if I could ask you a favor. I want to get a student's perspective on something she wrote, someone who knows her, to see if I'm going crazy."

If Principal Horowitz was trying to put me at ease, it wasn't working. He slid the stack of papers toward me. "Please tell me what you think. And be honest. This isn't a test."

Now I *was* jumpy. I knew I shouldn't have started gambling at lunch. How could *I* possibly judge anything Samara Brooks wrote? We weren't best friends or anything. We'd hardly hung out before this year. I even owed her money. Something was definitely wrong. Principal Horowitz was a nice guy, but he never asked students for favors.

"Um . . . I'll try." I grudgingly started flipping through the pages.

HYPOTHESIS: SAMARA BROOKS AND LILY FREDERICK ARE THE SAME, AND IF THEY ARE THE SAME, THEY SHOULD BE TREATED THE SAME, RIGHT?

A SCIENTIFIC STUDY
BY SAMARA BROOKS

Greetings, esteemed teachers and faculty of Madison Middle School!

In this experiment I intend to prove that there is *no difference* between Lily Frederick and myself at the atomic level.

We both have the exact same kind of DNA, which makes us both human. Lily and I may behave differently, but this has nothing to do with our innate makeup. I don't even wear makeup. Get it? ☺ That was a joke, by the way. It's not part of the hypothesis. I think science should be fun, so I try to lighten up my experiments.

Section A: Criteria, or How the Hypothesis Works

How does a scientific hypothesis work? It must be testable and falsifiable.

(Hopefully by answering that question I'm showing you that I know what I'm doing. And I realize I'm employing the Socratic method a lot here, but please bear with me.)

First, I will test my hypothesis by examining the cells of Lily Frederick and myself under the school's electron microscope. I will collect these cells by yanking a single strand of hair from Lily's head, and then yanking a single strand from my own head. Each strand will contain DNA with certain unique patterns, like fingerprints. So they may look a little different. But I aim to show that the *genetic structure* of our DNA is identical, which proves we are the same.

In every good scientific experiment, there must be a "control," which helps falsify a flawed hypothesis. Therefore, I am also going to ask Lily's mother to donate a strand of hair.

If there are big differences between my unique DNA and the unique DNA of Lily and her mother, then my hypothesis will be proven false. Since we know Lily is a nice, good person, then this might even be cause for concern. It could even hint at the presence of an "evil gene" in me that makes me a bad person. Yikes!

Section B: Authentication, or Proving I Am Not
Full of Crap

To make sure things go smoothly, I'll ask Principal Horowitz and Mrs. Belle to supervise the entire experiment. In addition, I propose we bring in Dr. Belle from the Madison Police Department to help us, as we could probably use all the help we can get. Hopefully Mrs. Belle will have figured out how to use the microscope by then, too.

Section C: Conclusion

If Dr. Belle and Mrs. Belle agree that there is no difference in the genetic makeup of the three samples of hair, then I will have proved my hypothesis: Lily Frederick and I are both the exact same kind of human beings, neither good nor bad. Therefore: No need to call my parents about my lunchtime casino. On the other hand, if we do discover big differences, or in a worst-case scenario the presence of an "evil gene," the police will be there to haul me away. ☺

With all due humility,
Samara Brooks

When I finished, I was more confused than ever. Principal Horowitz was staring at me. I could hear his watch ticking.

"So, what do you think?" he said.

"Um . . . it's funny?" I suggested.

"Anything else?"

I thought for a minute. "Well, let's see. I don't think there's such a thing as an evil gene. I think she's right about the Socratic method, though.[2] That's, like, asking a question as a way of teaching, right?" I paused. "Is this a joke?"

"Do *you* think it's a joke, Nathan?" Principal Horowitz asked, firing the Socratic method right back at me.

"Umm . . ." I was stuck. Fortunately, before I could make a complete fool out of myself, the library door flew open, and Samara Brooks strode in.

"Principal Horowitz! Did you get my e-mail?" She didn't bother with hello. It might have been a question, but she didn't deliver it like one. She delivered it like a news report. She yanked out a chair—the one beside mine—and sat down. Her black hair hung in her face. She brushed it from her eyes and smiled across the table. I sat frozen, unable to keep from staring at the mole next to her nose.

"Yes, I did, Samara," Principal Horowitz answered dryly. "Hello to you, too."

"Sorry. Hi. So, what do you think? Are we good to go this afternoon?"

---

[2] Socrates was a famous philosopher who lived in Greece twenty-five hundred years ago. He was forced to drink poison hemlock for corrupting young minds with his beliefs, which included his belief in aliens. Lots of people don't know that about Socrates. It's true, though. You can look it up.

"Well, I wanted to discuss it with you first." Principal Horowitz nodded toward me. "And since Nathan is here, I figured we'd include him in this conversation as well. As a control."

Samara furrowed her brow. "Why should Nathan Weiss be included? I mean, no offense, but my hypothesis includes all the major players."

Principal Horowitz smiled. "It's funny that you should use the word *players*, Samara. Because I'm trying to determine if you're attempting to . . ."

"Con you?" she finished.

He chuckled. "The word I'd use is *bluff*. But you're on the right track."

"Excuse me," I interrupted as politely as I could. "I'm sorry to cut in, but it sounds like this is really none of my business." I heaved my backpack over my shoulder and stood, nearly falling over my chair. "I'll just—"

At that very moment, Principal Horowitz's cell phone rang. He yanked it out of his jacket pocket and grimaced at the number. "Sorry, I have to take this," he muttered. He jumped up and rushed toward the library exit. "You two stay put."

Samara swiveled toward me. "Why did Principal Horowitz call you in here? What's he up to?"

"God only knows," I mumbled. I sat back down.

"Perfect. So I shouldn't ask Principal Horowitz? I should ask God?"

"No— I—I mean, I—"

"I'm joking with you, Nathan." She smirked.

"Oh. Well, Principal Horowitz didn't call me in, if that's what you're wondering. He knew I'd be in the library because—"

"You're about to crack a medieval code that proves aliens exist," she said.

My face reddened. "I, well, I mean . . . yeah, but that doesn't have anything to do with it. Anyway, I don't really believe in God," I blurted out, as if that might help.

"Oh." She slumped back into her seat. "You don't believe in God. How nice."

I frowned at her. "Why? Does that offend you?"

"Hardly. Nothing offends me. But let me tell you something, Nathan. At a school like this, you have to play the odds." She peeked over her shoulder toward the exit, and then lowered her voice. "Even if God doesn't exist, a lot of people around here think he does. So that makes him real. Get it?"

"Not really," I said, annoyed.

"My point is that telling someone around here that you *don't* believe in God isn't a wise move," she said. "Odds are that sooner or later you'll offend somebody who believes he does. You got lucky with me, that's all. Just a bit of helpful advice."

"Thanks," I said.

"No problem."

"I have to tell you, though, Samara, that's the dumbest thing I've ever heard," I said. "How can telling the truth ever be bad?"

She sniffed. "I didn't say it could. What's bad is telling the *whole* truth."

I rolled my eyes. "Now you're not making any sense at all—"

"Sorry!" Principal Horowitz called to us, shambling back to the table. He shoved his phone back into his pocket. For what seemed like a long time, he gazed at us blankly, as if he had no idea who Samara and I were or why we were all sitting together in the library at 7:35 in the morning.

"I'm sorry," he repeated. "I'm a little distracted. I always turn my cell off at eight o'clock to avoid personal . . ." He swallowed. "Right. Time for you two to get to your classes. Everything seems in order here. Samara, I'd like you to conduct your experiment after school today. We'll find out then if it's a joke or not."

"Do you need me to be there, too?" I asked. *Please say no. Please say no—*

"Good idea, Nathan," he answered without missing a beat. "Thanks for offering. We could use another pair of eyes. I've e-mailed Lily and her mother . . ." He shook his head, as if losing his train of thought. "Dr. Belle from the Madison

Police Department will be joining us, too. And last evening, Mrs. Belle called to say that she spoke with someone who finally helped her figure out how to use the microscope . . . so we're all set. Sound good, kids?"

Kids? I glanced at Samara. Principal Horowitz never called us kids.

He slapped the table with his palms. "Great!" he proclaimed, flashing a big fake smile. With that, he hopped up and hurried out the door.

"That was weird," Samara said once we had a chance to collect ourselves.

"This whole morning has been weird," I mumbled. I was surprised Principal Horowitz was going along with Samara's plan. And what were the chances that Mrs. Belle would have finally figured out how to use the microscope last night?

"Don't you think Principal Horowitz is acting sort of funny? He keeps rambling."

"Yeah," I said. "He's jumpy, too."

"I wonder if it has anything to do with his wife," she said.

My ears perked up. "What do you mean?"

Samara drummed her fingers on the table. She peered back toward the exit. "I heard his wife left him this summer," she whispered.

"Really?" *Wow*. I felt bad for him. I'd never thought of him as an actual person before, a regular guy who existed outside school. "I didn't even know he had a wife."

"Yeah, well, you've never been to the principal's office." She fidgeted in her seat. "Okay, look, Nathan. Can I tell you something? I mean, I know you probably don't think I'm the greatest person to begin with. But when I was writing this hypothesis last night, I asked my brother if he had any dirt I could use on Principal Horowitz."

I drew back. "You did?"

"Hey, I'm sorry, all right?" she muttered defensively. "I'm trying to make a confession. Whatever. It's terrible, I know. But I wanted to cover my bets. See, Jim used to get called to the principal's office a lot, too, when he went to school here. And he's a pretty nosy guy. I wondered if he'd ever poked around where he shouldn't have."

"Did he?" I asked.

"Not then. But get this: A few days ago, he randomly bumped into Principal Horowitz in my dad's law office." She leaned closer. "Totally by coincidence. Jim said Principal Horowitz pretended not to see him at first. And when he did, he acted all embarrassed. See, my dad's firm specializes in divorces. It turns out—"

"It's okay, Samara," I interrupted. "Say no more. I get the

picture." Not only did I get the picture; it was bleakly familiar. My parents had recently gotten divorced, too. And if Principal Horowitz's divorce was turning out to be anything like theirs, then I felt *really* bad for him. I pushed myself away from the table, wishing I hadn't come to school early for once. "Listen, Samara, I should probably get going. Class starts in . . ." My eyes wandered to the clock above the checkout desk. It was 7:40. Class didn't start for another twenty minutes.

"Where are you rushing off to?" Samara asked with a lop-sided grin. "I thought you said you liked to come to the library early. You know, because you're about to crack a code that proves aliens exist." She sounded as if she were talking to a three-year-old.

"Samara, I . . ." My voice petered out.

"Nathan, I'll tell you what. I'll make you a deal. If you tell me about this medieval code, I'll forget about the twelve bucks you owe me."

I hesitated. "You will?"

"Yeah. But you have to explain it to me in a way that I can actually understand."

I blinked at her several times. I couldn't tell if she was being serious or not. I could *never* tell.

"Come on." She wriggled her eyebrows. "It's a sweet deal."

I weighed the pros and cons.

The pros: I'd be out of debt, which meant I could quit gambling in the cafeteria for good. I'd stop carrying cash and start packing my own lunches, just to avoid the temptation.

The cons: This was a big conversation, and one that I definitely wasn't in the mood for. Also, no matter what I said, I had a feeling she'd use it as ammunition to rag on me until the end of the year—and possibly for the rest of our lives.

Just as I was about to bolt, there was a commotion at the library door.

"Hi, Nathan!" Mrs. Belle called out. "Oh, good. I'm glad Principal Horowitz was able to let you in. I've been held up in the lab. Hi, Samara!"

"Hi, Mrs. Belle!" Samara called back.

Mrs. Belle scurried toward us, her tote bag bumping against her side. In general she's a little messier and more disorganized than most teachers, but this was the first time I'd seen dust bunnies clinging to her white lab coat. She looked as if she'd been rummaging around in an attic somewhere.

"Good news!" she announced. "The electron microscope is officially working! Well, knock on wood." She rapped her knuckles against the table. "Samara, Principal Horowitz told me about your experiment last night, so I wanted to make sure everything was good to go. He forwarded me your hypothesis early this morning. What a neat idea! Using your DNA to prove that you and Lily Frederick are the same! Very clever."

"Thanks," Samara said. "I'm glad you think so. I can't wait to see the fabulous electron microscope in action."

"And I can't wait to show you the console and monitor," Mrs. Belle replied. "I've just been firing up all the different components, and I had to crawl around on the lab floor to find enough outlets. There are so many different parts—" She broke off, glancing between the two of us. "Sorry. Looks like I'm interrupting something."

"Actually, Nathan was just telling me about this mysterious ancient code he's researching," Samara piped up.

"It's the, uh, Voynich Manuscript," I mumbled when Mrs. Belle looked at me.

"Do you know anything about it, Mrs. Belle?" Samara asked.

Uh-oh.

"Oh, yes!" Mrs. Belle plopped down into Principal Horowitz's vacant chair. The dust bunnies floated off into the book stacks.

Samara glanced at me, her eyes twinkling. "Hey, where are you going, Nathan? Have a seat."

I slumped back down at the table. I wondered if after all

70

this, Samara would still make me pay my gambling debt. (Honestly, who knew *what* she was thinking?) And I like Mrs. Belle—she's nice and all—but she does tend to talk and talk and talk.

"Well, the Voynich Manuscript is a six-hundred-year-old riddle," Mrs. Belle said. "It's a book, or a codex, that was handwritten sometime during the fifteenth century. The most amazing thing about it is that nobody can decipher its language. Even professional cryptologists, people who crack spy codes, can't figure out what it means."

"Wow," Samara said. "Is that really true?"

I had to give Samara credit: If she was pretending to be curious, she was doing a pretty good job.

"It is," Mrs. Belle replied. "The manuscript is quite beautiful, too. Very intricate. It's illustrated with all sorts of wild, beautiful drawings, mostly of plants and flowers. And charts. Some contain faces. They mostly follow a similar circular eyelike pattern, almost like a wheel or the zodiac. You have to see it to believe it." She gestured toward the library's computer center. "I can show you some pictures of it online, if you'd like."

"Sure, that would be great," Samara said. "But, hey, let me ask you something. Do you think it might prove that aliens exist?"

Mrs. Belle chuckled. "Well, who's to say? Human beings certainly haven't had much luck figuring out what it's trying to tell us." She winked at Samara and turned to me. "I will say this: Like Nathan, I do love trying to solve riddles and crack codes, too. Which reminds me, Nathan, have you had any luck solving the riddle I gave you?"

I could feel my face turning red again. *Did you have to bring that up?* The first day back at school, Mrs. Belle had presented me with a riddle that contained a code. And, yes, I admit it; I hadn't had any luck figuring it out. And no, I didn't much feel like sharing this little bit of information with anyone, especially not Samara Brooks.

"What's the riddle?" Samara asked eagerly.

"It's called Skipping on All Fours," Mrs. Belle said. "I'll give you a hint first. Only one in four counts if you're trying to make sense."

"One in four," Samara said. "Okeydokey."

"Right. Now pay close attention." Mrs. Belle smiled coyly. "Fill in ten big dots. Tip the stew. Tuck in open drapes. Do not powwow."

Samara waited for more. "That's it?"

"That's it."

"Is there some secret message or something I'm missing?" Samara asked.

"Well, if I told you, then I'd be giving away the riddle, right?" Mrs. Belle teased.

"You got me there," Samara said. "Nathan, you really can't figure it out?"

"Well, I haven't really tried that hard," I lied. The truth was that it had been driving me crazy. I was beginning to wish that I were somewhere else—anywhere but here. "Hey, I just remembered . . . I have to call my mom. I mean, she told me to call her when I got to school." *Ugh.* The lie sounded even less convincing out loud than it had in my head. I leapt out of my seat. "Sorry."

"Wait, Nathan!" Mrs. Belle reached into her tote bag and pulled out a crumpled magazine page. "I brought something that I thought you might find interesting. It's an article about another ancient riddle, the Phaistos Disk." She waved it in front of me. "Are you familiar with it?"

"Um . . . maybe I've heard of it once or twice," I said.[3]

---

[3] That's not true, either. I'd spent most of the summer reading about it. The Phaistos Disk is a thirty-five-hundred-year-old bronze wheel about the size of a coffee saucer, discovered in Greece. It's carved with forty-five different symbols, the very last of which looks exactly like the eye-shaped designs found in the Voynich Manuscript. Archaeologists believe it might be a farmer's almanac: a guide to planting crops based on which stars are in the sky. Some believe the Voynich Manuscript might be a farmer's almanac, too. This may sound boring, but it will be important later on. Trust me on this.

"I think you'll find the article fascinating!" Mrs. Belle said.

"Thanks," I mumbled. I shoved the paper into my back pocket and stole a sidelong glance at Samara. She chewed on her cheek, trying not to laugh.

I really did appreciate that Mrs. Belle was so nice to me all the time. But I vowed right then and there to stop coming to the library every single morning.

As I hurried out the door, I couldn't help but turn the strange words over in my head for the zillionth time.

Fill in ten big dots. Tip the stew. Tuck in open drapes. Do not powwow.

Gibberish. That's what it sounded like. Complete gibberish. It didn't even rhyme. The hint didn't help, either. Only one in four counted if I was trying to make sense? Which one? Tip the stew? And why was it called Skipping on All Fours?

I had a lousy feeling that I wouldn't ever be able to crack whatever code was hidden in that riddle. I also had a lousy feeling that when Mrs. Belle finally explained it to me, the answer would be totally obvious, and I'd feel like a complete idiot.

The lousiest feeling of all, though, was that Samara Brooks would somehow manage to be right there when Mrs. Belle gave the answer away—with a big smile on her face, getting a kick out of it all.

Part Three
Lily Frederick

So first I guess I should tell you what I think about God, to be fair to Samara and Nathan. I believe that God can answer our prayers. Maybe that sounds corny, but I really do. He might not answer them in a way that we expect, but he'll always answer them in a way that helps. I know, because I'd been praying for help pretty much nonstop ever since I checked my e-mail that Friday morning, right up until Aunt Esther pulled up in her blue hybrid to take me to school.

Dear God,

I never should have started playing blackjack.

I went online again last night to read up on it, even though Mom and Dad don't like me to be online so late. Bad idea. I found out that gambling is something you can get hooked on. It's like eating candy or playing video games or surfing the Web too much.

The more I read, God, the worse it sounded. The problem gamblers were the scariest of all. This one guy said he ended up owing $78,564.46 on eight different credit cards. He said he felt like he didn't have any power over gambling. He said he felt as if it had been written into his DNA, like the color of his eyes!

That last line really killed me. Written into his DNA???

I almost wanted to wake up Mom and Dad and show them the

link. But I knew I'd get into trouble. I don't understand them at all sometimes. Don't you think it's wrong that they're flying off to Vegas again this morning? I'm so confused. And I know I shouldn't gamble, but who would have ever thought that Samara Brooks would set up a casino in the cafeteria? Temptation really is everywhere, like they say in church.

Anyway, God, if you see your way to doing me one small favor, I promise I'll give up gambling for good.

Can you make sure Mom and Dad forget to check their e-mail this morning?

I know it's a lot to ask, God, and this is all my fault, but I'm in a tough spot here.

So, I guess that's it. Thank you. And thank you for all the excellent blessings you've given me. Thank you for helping me win the election last spring, and for making me class president. Thank you for giving me the mom and dad I have, even though I do get mad at them sometimes. Most of all, thanks for listening, like always.

"Lily?" Mom called from downstairs. "Time to go! Aunt Esther's here!"

"Okay, be right down!" I called shakily. I wasn't sure I could move. I'd been stuck in my desk chair for going on ten minutes straight, staring at the e-mail on my computer screen.

77

From: horowitz@mms.edu
To: LilyFrederickprez@mms.edu
Date: September 6
Subject: Madison Middle School asks permission to examine your DNA

Hi, Lily.

After much thought, I've decided not to discipline you for skipping English class yesterday. Until now your record has been spotless, so I trust you'll make it to all your classes in the future.

I do wish you would stop playing card games in the cafeteria, however, which is why I'm writing. Originally I faulted Samara Brooks for the trouble these games are causing. As you know, Samara is a very bright student who likes to bend the rules. But she has agreed to stop the games.

To make a long story short, she crafted a smart if somewhat nutty scientific experiment to prove that she's not a bad person any more than you are. She feels the blame for the trouble should be shared equally between you two, or not at all. Her theory is that you and she are exactly the same. She wants to examine your DNA to prove this, with our help.

In spite of my reservations, Samara's experiment does provide Madison Middle School with a chance for students to use our electron microscope.

So I ask that you join us in the science lab after classes today, at 3:00 p.m. Be prepared to stay until 3:30, if you can. Please bring a strand of your hair to be examined. We can pluck it there if you like. I've also e-mailed your mother and asked her to provide a strand of hair, too. I know this might sound a bit worrisome and confusing, but you shouldn't be concerned. It's all in good fun, and hopefully we can all learn something from it! It's best to turn an unfortunate episode into something positive whenever possible, don't you agree?

I'll explain the experiment in greater detail this afternoon. See you then!

79

Thanks in advance,
Principal Horowitz

"Lily?" Mom's voice rose. "Come on, honey! You don't want to be late!"

Aunt Esther honked her horn.

"Coming!" I buried my face in my hands, then jabbed my finger at the power button. The computer winked off. As I stood, I caught a glimpse of my reflection in the monitor. *Oh no. Look at me, God*, I thought. *Look at those sacks under my eyes. That's the way Mom and Dad look whenever they get back from a trip to Vegas!*

Maybe it was a sign. Maybe I was doomed to gamble my life down the drain.

I grabbed my backpack and slunk down the stairs. Mom and Dad were waiting by the front door, dressed in the same matching blue nylon tracksuits they always wear when they're about to head off to the airport. Mom held up a little white envelope.

My heart beat faster. "What's that?"

She smiled. "It's a strand of my hair for you to take to school!"

"Oh, right." I gulped.

"Weren't you just checking your e-mail?" Dad asked. "Didn't Principal Horowitz write to you this morning?"

I nodded queasily. "He wrote to you guys, too, huh?"

"Yes, he did!" Mom chirped. "He wanted our permission for you to participate in the experiment this afternoon. And I think it's such a neat idea! Examining your DNA! It's so grown-up! You're so lucky to go to Madison Middle School, you know that?"

"Um, I guess I am." I blinked several times.

"Make sure someone takes lots of pictures," Dad said. "I wish we could be there to see the whole shebang ourselves."

Something wasn't quite adding up. "You guys aren't upset?" I managed.

Mom and Dad glanced at each other, puzzled.

"No," Mom said.

"Why should we be?" Dad asked.

I stared at them. "What did Principal Horowitz say in the e-mail, exactly?"

Mom tilted her head. "Just that he needed a strand of hair from one of us, and that you'd be supplying one, too. For an experiment that one of your friends dreamed up."

"Right," Dad said. "And that the experiment would

provide the school with its first historic opportunity to use the electron microscope."

I began to relax. "That's it?"

"That's it," she said.

Amazing. There was only one explanation. Principal Horowitz had decided not to mention anything to my parents about my gambling problem or cutting English class. For whatever reason, he'd let me off the hook.

Thank you, God, I said silently, taking the envelope from Mom's hand. *Thank you for answering my prayers, again.*

Aunt Esther must have grown tired of waiting in the car, because she marched right up the front walk, chomping loudly on a piece of bubble gum.

"Ready to go, Lily?" She glowered at Mom and Dad. "Got everything you need for the weekend?" she asked me.

I nodded. "Yup. It's all in my backpack."

"Good." Aunt Esther's bubble gum smacked against her lips. "You know what gets me?"

"What's that?" I asked.

"These two deadbeats would rather get an extra-early start to Vegas than drive their own daughter, the class president, to school."

I cringed. "It's really not a big deal," I told her, hoping to avoid an argument.

"We're not deadbeats," Mom said, frowning at Esther. "We've had this trip planned for a while now. Lily knows. She also knows how proud of her we are. Right, Lily?"

Dad smiled at me. "You're first in *our* class, too."

Aunt Esther snorted. "Then why do you two always do this?"

"What do you mean?" Dad said.

"Why do you tell your daughter that children should never gamble, and then jet off to Vegas?" she demanded.

"Because children *shouldn't* gamble," Mom said. "And because Vegas is fun and relaxing. For adults."

"If it's so fun and relaxing, then why do you always look like garbage when you get back?" she practically shouted.

Aunt Esther was right. And normally I don't like to ruffle anyone's feathers if I can help it—least of all Mom and Dad's—but for once I mustered the courage to speak up. "It's true, you guys," I murmured. "You always end up taking Monday off from work and sleeping the whole day."

"Amen," Aunt Esther muttered under her breath.

"How about we discuss this when we get back, okay?" Dad said with the same bright smile he'd been wearing all morning. He stepped forward and patted me on the back, nudging me out the door. "We need to be getting to the airport, and Lily, you need to be getting to school. Have fun with the experiment."

"And good luck!" Mom added.

Dad reached for the doorknob. "We'll call you as soon as we get to the hotel, to let you know we got there safe."

"Have a great weekend, honey!" Mom said, blowing me a kiss. "We love you!"

The front door slammed.

Aunt Esther popped a loud bubble.

"I'll tell you what, Lily," she said. "How about we skip church this Sunday and have some fun of our own?"

Once we'd pulled out of our little cul-de-sac and onto the main road, Aunt Esther flipped on her favorite morning radio show: *Gettin' Gospel*.

A big reason Aunt Esther likes *Gettin' Gospel* so much is because she knows the show's host, Dr. Willis. Well, not super-personally or anything, but enough to say hi. He gives the sermons at Church of the Shepherd. You might have even seen him on TV; his services are broadcast all across the country. I'd go so far as to say that he's kind of a celebrity. He looks like one, at least: graying, smooth, and dashing.

Every week Dr. Willis packs the pews with hot spotlights

and cameramen who swivel around on cranes, plus a bunch of assistants in headsets who stand in the aisles and encourage the congregation to applaud.

I have to admit, it's pretty neat to go to church on the set of a real live TV show. People actually wait in line to get seats. Luckily, Aunt Esther is a regular contributor, so she always has tickets.

Dr. Willis's deep voice hummed in the car speakers. "Good day, friends. Today's theme is the miracle of hidden messages. The Bible is full of them."

I tried to ease back in the cushions. Dr. Willis's voice can be very relaxing.

"I'd like to talk for a bit about a Commandment we tend to take at face value," he went on. "'Honor thy father and thy mother.' Pretty straightforward, right? How can the words mean anything more than what's written?"

Aunt Esther reached over and lowered the volume. "Sorry. We can listen to something else if you like."

"I don't mind," I said.

"I just figured you might not be in the mood for a lesson about honoring your father and mother right now." She winked at me.

I shrugged. "Maybe there's a hidden message about something more."

"Remember, friends: The Bible is like an onion," Dr. Willis was saying. "An onion made of gold, with a diamond at its center."

Aunt Esther chuckled. "Onions make me cry," she mused. "No wonder I have such a hard time understanding the Bible sometimes."

"Do you really?" I asked.

"Don't you?" She raised her shoulders, her gaze fixed on the road. "It's hard enough with all the strange names, like Zebulun and Methuselah and Nebuchadnezzar. And don't get me started on the places. The language gives me a headache. I mean, it's hardly written the way people talk nowadays. Some of it is just so strange and stilted."

I swallowed, feeling uncomfortable. "Well, some of the Bible is like poetry," I pointed out. "Your name comes from the Bible, right?"

"Oh, I know, Lily." She shot me a quick smile. "But you want to know the truth? Sometimes I get more out of a book like *Chicken Soup for the Soul* than I do out of the Bible. Everything there is spelled right out for me. No 'thou shalts' or 'begats' or 'speaketh.' No hidden messages. Just the way I like it. But that's just me." She winked at me again. "It could be that I'm lazy."

I stared at the traffic whizzing past in the opposite

direction. If Aunt Esther was lazy, then I was even lazier. I didn't like to admit it, but the Bible *was* confusing. The parts I liked the most were the parts that were most like stories—like when Jesus marches into the temple and overturns all the moneylenders' tables, making a huge mess. *"Don't be afraid to defy authority!"* Dr. Willis had once preached about that very passage. *"Jesus was a rebel, too!"* Every now and then, those words would pop into my head, even when I wasn't in church. Deep down, I wondered if they had something to do with why I took Samara Brooks up on her offer to gamble.

"God's got his eye on us, friends," Dr. Willis continued. "He's watching us peel that onion. He's watching all the time, helping us along . . ."

"You want to know something, Lily?" Aunt Esther said gently.

"What's that?"

"You worry too much for someone so young." She turned off the radio, then leaned over and patted my knee. "Not everything contains a hidden message. Some things are just as you see them."

No matter how hard I tried that day, I couldn't sneak in a nap. Two sleepless nights were finally catching up with me. I spent lunch in the library, hoping to snooze with my head down at an empty desk, but people kept wandering over and tapping me on the shoulder to see if I was all right. The attention was nice, but for once I almost wished I weren't class president. People used to leave me alone a lot more before I won the election last year. By the time the final bell rang, I was light-headed, not to mention starving. Skipping lunch was a lousy idea.

"Feel better, Lily!" Wendy Melvin called as she rushed past me down the hall into the afternoon sunshine. "See you for blackjack Monday, right? Have a great weekend!"

If I can make it past three-thirty, I thought glumly, trudging toward the science lab.

I'm not a huge fan of the science lab to begin with. It's always too cold, and the air reeks of rubbing alcohol and air freshener. Today it smelled even worse than usual. I caught a whiff of the antiseptic odor halfway down the hall.

"Hey, Lily!" Samara yelled through the open door. "Just in time!"

I paused outside.

Crowded around the microscope with Samara were Nathan Weiss, Principal Horowitz, and Mrs. Belle. Plus there was a bespectacled doctor type in a white lab coat that matched Mrs. Belle's, two uniformed policemen—one chubby, one thin—and a peculiar-looking gray-haired woman in a colorful dress and a crystal necklace the size of a bicycle chain.

"Ready to see what my DNA looks like?" Samara asked with a sly smile. She waved a pair of tweezers at me. "I just put my hair on the slide."

"Um, sure," I said. My voice was hoarse. I wondered who all the strangers were.

Principal Horowitz stepped toward me. "Lily, are you all right? You seem tired."

"I'm fine." I rubbed my eyes, trying to shake off the dizziness.

"Did something at lunch disagree with you?" he asked, sounding worried.

"Actually, I never made it to lunch," I confessed. As if on cue, my stomach growled. My baffled gaze wandered to the two policemen, then to the doctor type, then to the woman in the dress . . . and finally to Mrs. Belle, who sat hunched in front of the electron microscope's computer screen. A small row of red lights blinked beneath it.

What a weird machine, I thought. Until today, the whole apparatus had always struck me as sort of comical—like it could have come straight out of a dingy thrift store, or an old grainy reel-to-reel film. The drab beige plastic reminded me of the furniture in Aunt Esther's den. She'd inherited my grandparents' house and never redecorated. But now the microscope equipment sort of gave me the creeps.

"Everybody ready?" Mrs. Belle asked. "Here we go . . ."

She flicked a switch—then came a loud *O-O-O-H-M.*

I gulped at the sound. Part of me had been secretly hoping that it wouldn't work. A fuzzy black-and-white image flickered to life on the screen, vibrating and wormlike. My pulse picked up a notch.

"What *is* that?" I croaked over the hum of the generator.

"That's my DNA," Samara replied proudly.

I peered at it a little closer. "Why is it so shaky?"

"Maybe because I was so nervous when I pulled out my hair," she joked. "For all I know, I *do* have an evil gene. Ha!"

I blinked at the tweezers clutched in her hand.

"Lily, the image is shaking like that because we're seeing DNA at its atomic level!" Mrs. Belle explained cheerily, as if that would somehow make me feel better. "Atoms are constantly in motion."

"Yes, you're looking at Samara's hair magnified four hundred and eighty thousand times," Principal Horowitz added. "We're about to snap a picture of it, and then the microscope will produce a photo negative, which we'll print later."

"Then it's your turn," Samara said. She pinched the tweezers in the air.

Fear crept over me. *If gambling is built into my DNA, like that gambling guy said on the Internet, then I bet it will somehow show up on that screen. I bet my DNA will shake even more than Samara's because I'm even more nervous than she is—*

"Hey, Lily, are you sure you're okay?" Samara whispered.

I managed a feeble nod.

"If you're not feeling well, we really don't have to do this," she said so no one else could hear. "Seriously. We can call the whole thing off."

"No, no, that's okay," I answered unconvincingly. "But do you mind if I ask a question? Why are the police here?"

The doctor type in the glasses and lab coat overheard and strode forward, extending a hand. "I'll answer that, Lily," he said with a smile. "I apologize. I should have introduced myself earlier. I'm Dr. Samuel Belle, the resident forensic scientist at the Madison Police Department. My wife is your science teacher." He gestured toward Mrs. Belle, and then at the two policemen. "And these men are Detectives Rosen and Gulden. I figured they might want to see a demonstration of DNA analysis. I hope that's all right?"

"Sure, of course." I forced myself to shake his hand. "Nice to meet you, Dr. Belle. And you, too, Detectives."

"And I'm Nathan Weiss's mom," the gray-haired woman with the clunky necklace said. "I wanted to see this famous electron microscope for myself before I take him home."

"Oh. Well, nice to meet . . . to meet . . ."

My lips kept working in little spasms, but no sound would come out. My heart pounded. The floor spun beneath my feet. I clutched the doorframe for support. *Maybe we* should *call the whole thing off,* I thought. Yes. Good decision. I wanted to say so, but a *whoosh* filled my ears, and a purplish haze swept over the room. My field of vision shrank until I saw nothing but the shaky black-and-white worm on the video screen.

"Hey, did you remember to bring a strand of your mom's hair?" Samara asked.

Her voice sounded far away, as if she were calling across a wide canyon. Before I could answer, the floor seemed to open up and swallow me whole.

When I came to, Samara was cradling my head in her hands. My eyelashes fluttered. It took a few seconds for my blurry vision to melt into focus.

Everyone was still huddled around the electron microscope's video monitor.

"Hello?" Samara barked. "Anybody home? Lily passed out, in case you hadn't noticed! A little help?"

The cold tile floor felt strangely soothing beneath my back. Samara's hands made a nice pillow, too.

"Goodness!" Nathan's mom exclaimed. She tore herself from the screen and kneeled beside Samara, her big crystal necklace bumping against my cheek. "Sorry, Lily. What kind of people are we? Let me look at you. Your pupils don't seem dilated."

"Is that good or bad?" I croaked. My throat was dry. I sounded like a frog.

Principal Horowitz rushed over. "I'm sorry, Lily. I didn't even see what happened. There was something surprising on the video screen. . . ."

"More surprising than one of your own students keeling over?" Samara asked in a flat voice.

"Of course not," Principal Horowitz murmured apologetically. He hopped up and tapped the chubby policeman on the shoulder. I wasn't sure if it was Rosen or Gulden. I couldn't remember which was which. "The school nurse is gone for the day, so let's call nine-one-one and get Lily to the hospital as soon as possible. I'll notify her parents."

"No!" I cried.

Everyone turned to me.

"I mean, no, really, I'm fine," I said groggily. I forced myself to sit up straight. I tried to smile, even though the room started spinning again and my lips felt like sandpaper. "I don't want to be a bother. Anyway, my parents are out of town. My aunt Esther will be here any minute. She'll take me home."

"Are you sure, Lily?" Samara asked.

I nodded several times fast. If Principal Horowitz notified my parents, then they would want to know the whole story—which meant sooner or later I would have to admit that I'd agreed to take part in this little experiment to get off the hook for gambling. And there was no way (none!) I could let my parents find out about *that*. Because that would also mean confessing that I'd been keeping a terrible secret from them. That would mean confessing that I owed Samara Brooks sixty-three dollars.

"Lily, you're shaking," Nathan Weiss's mom said, concerned.

"Am I? I'm just a little chilly. It's chilly in here, isn't it? Maybe that's why Samara's DNA is shaking, too. Ha . . . Get it? It's shaking because it's . . ." I didn't finish. It probably wasn't a good idea to attempt any humor.

"It *is* chilly," Nathan agreed. "I say we go to the library and try to get some answers. It's warmer in there."

"Nathan, please," his mom groaned. "One of your classmates is lying on the floor. We're not about to leave her here."

"But she says she's all right. I mean . . . I'm sorry, Lily, but you all saw what I saw, right? This is crazy! This is nuts! This is totally . . . extraordinary!"

Mrs. Belle and her husband exchanged a worried glance.

"What's extraordinary?" I said.

Nathan stepped over me and hurried out the door. "There's something in Samara's DNA! It looks exactly like the eye symbols in the Phaistos Disk and the Voynich Manuscript! It could be some kind of message, or part of a code! Don't you think so, Mrs. Belle?"

Mrs. Belle laughed nervously. "Well, let's not jump to conclusions."

Good idea, I thought. Just listening to Nathan made me tired and foggy again. Those funny names he'd mentioned made me think of Aunt Esther, too, and why she thought the Bible was too complicated sometimes. Probably best to tune out. I leaned back in Samara's hands.

"What are you saying, exactly, Nathan?" Principal Horowitz asked.

"Yeah, are you saying that I'm an alien?" Samara called after him.

"That's what I want to find out!" His footsteps clattered down the hall. "I think we could have just made a huge discovery! I'll be in the library, okay? Sorry, Lily! Feel better!"

Samara looked down at me. In spite of everything, I giggled. Only Nathan Weiss could make the possibility of discovering that someone was an alien sound like the happiest moment of his life—and even better, like it could be true.

Nathan's mom cleared her throat. "Well. Now that we have a moment, I'd like to take this opportunity to apologize for my son. I wish I could say that he doesn't normally behave like this. But then I'd be lying to you."

For the next few minutes, all the grown-ups debated among themselves about what to do with me. A trip to the emergency room? A ride home? Should they call my parents now? Call my parents later? I hoisted myself to my feet, clinging to Samara for support. *Please, God, none of the above,* I prayed silently. I was half tempted to follow Nathan's example and bolt, when somebody knocked on the open door: a tall, skinny, vaguely familiar-looking older boy with a mop of curly red hair.

"Hey, everyone," he said. "What's going on?"

Samara leaned over and whispered in his ear for a few seconds.

He nodded, then stepped over and seized my wrist. "Lily, is it? Hi, I'm Jim Brooks, Samara's brother. I understand you just fainted? Let me check your pulse."

"Uh . . ." Maybe my brain was still fuzzy, but time suddenly seemed to speed up, as if God had pressed a giant fast-forward button.

"Jim, it's nice to see you here, but there's no need to lend a hand," Principal Horowitz said in a dry voice. "We have the situation under control, thanks."

"Lily, your pulse is only slightly elevated, and your vitals are all okay," Jim stated as if he hadn't heard. "The important thing now is to hydrate you." He let go of my wrist and turned to the policemen. "Detectives, if you need to be somewhere, I can handle this from here on out. I took a paramedic course over the summer—I'm applying for a dual MD and PhD program—so I don't mind watching her until her aunt shows up. She'll be fine. This is a piece of cake compared to ambulance duty."

Principal Horowitz opened his mouth and then closed it. He was speechless. I couldn't blame him. So was I. Jim sounded even more grown-up than *he* did.

"If you all could give her a little room, too, that would be great," Jim added. "It's crowded in here. She could use some fresh air."

"Maybe somebody should check up on Nathan," Samara suggested.

"Good idea," Nathan's mom muttered. She patted me on

the shoulder on her way out of the lab. "I'm sorry, sweetheart. My son does tend to get a little carried away."

Mrs. Belle hurried after her. "I think we *all* got a little carried away," she said.

"To your son's credit, Mrs. Weiss, the image on the screen *was* extraordinary," Dr. Belle said, following close on his wife's heels. He beckoned to the policemen. They filed out behind him. "It did look almost exactly like an eye—with a tiny pupil at the center and an iris radiating from it."

Principal Horowitz frowned, watching as everyone vanished down the hall.

"Excuse me, Principal Horowitz?" Jim said. "Would you mind getting Lily some water? I'd get it myself, but I'd like to keep an eye on her."

"Well, um, I probably should stay, too," he stammered, sounding much less sure of himself than he had a minute ago.

"You don't have to," Jim insisted. He raised his eyebrows at me. "Lily?"

"Huh?" I said. "Oh—yes. I really am feeling much, much better. But some water would be great. Thanks."

Principal Horowitz bit his lip. "Okay," he said. "I'll be right back." He scurried out the door, shaking his head in bewilderment.

I let out a deep breath. Now that the grown-ups were gone, the lab felt a lot less claustrophobic. I wasn't on the verge of suffocating, or fainting again, either.

"Thanks, Jim," I said.

A smile flitted across his face.

Samara snickered.

"What's so funny?" I said.

"I think we owe Jim a round of applause," Samara said. "That was quite a performance. For years, he's studied at the feet of the master. And now, well, he's almost as good a con artist as I am."

"Almost?" He punched her arm.

"Ouch!" She punched him back.

My eyes widened. "What are you saying?"

"You don't really think I took a paramedic course, do you?" Jim asked.

"You made that up?" I cried.

Samara laughed. "Are you kidding? Ambulance duty? The guy turns green if he gets a paper cut."

He folded his arms across his chest. "Hardly. But I do hate hospitals."

I peered out the door. "I can't believe you lied like that to Principal Horowitz. And to Dr. and Mrs. Belle. And the police!"

"Don't forget Nathan's mom," Samara added.

I felt queasy.

Jim slouched against the doorframe. "Relax, Lily. It's not that big a deal. So I took a gamble. And the gamble paid off. Come on, did *you* want them to drag you off to the hospital?"

"I know *I* didn't," Samara said.

Neither did I, of course. Still, all the breezy talk of lying and conning and gambling scared me a little. Jim's kind of gambling wasn't like *my* kind of gambling. I gambled with cards. He'd gambled with people. On the other hand, who was I to judge? Maybe God had answered my prayers by sending Jim to bail me out. I could probably stand to learn from Jim—and from Samara, too. I'd made a lot of losing bets in the past few days, particularly on betting itself.

"What do you say we get out of here?" Samara suggested. "We can wait for your aunt Esther outside."

"Yeah, and if you want, I'll stay here and deal with Principal Horowitz when he gets back," Jim said. "I won't even lie. I'll tell him you went to meet your aunt."

I stole a quick peek at the electron microscope. The screen had gone dark. "What about the rest of the experiment?" I asked.

Samara chuckled and took my arm. "Don't worry, Lily,"

she soothed. "I think it's safe to say the experiment is over. You worry too much, you know that?"

"Okay." I plodded into the hall with her, too frazzled to protest. Maybe I *did* worry too much. I couldn't help it. My mind bubbled, a murky stew of random bits and pieces—of cons and lies, shaky DNA, and a debt of sixty-three dollars . . . and a final prayer that God might still forgive me for all the trouble I'd gotten myself into.

"Hey, Samara?" I said.

"Yeah?"

"What did everyone *really* see when I fainted? On the screen, I mean?"

"You know, I'm not really sure," she said. "Whatever it was, it didn't look like it belonged. Or at least, that's the idea I got from Dr. and Mrs. Belle."

"What do you think that means?" I asked.

"Who knows? *I* didn't put it there. I bet Nathan is hard at work cracking the code to get us the answer, though. Maybe I really do have an evil gene. Ha! Kidding."

"But . . . it looked like an eye?" I asked.

She thought for a moment. "I guess it did," she said.

I clung to her arm a little more tightly. I couldn't help thinking about Dr. Willis's sermon, and how he'd preached that God has his eye on us and is watching all the time. *God's eyes are everywhere,* I thought. Which meant Aunt Esther was wrong. There *were* hidden messages everywhere—even in the tiniest, hardest-to-find places in the universe. We just had to look for them. And when we did, we'd find God staring right back at us.

Which meant that Aunt Esther was wrong about something else, too. I had plenty of reason to worry. I just didn't have the slightest clue as to how much.

Part Four
Samara Brooks

Proof of Aliens

I conned my parents *way* more than usual over spaghetti and meatballs that night.

First, I told them about the big scientific experiment I dreamed up, and how thanks to my hypothesis, Madison Middle School finally broke in its "fabulous electron microscope." That got a big laugh. Then I told them about how Lily Frederick fainted, and how Jim and I took care of her. I even told them about the strange eye-thingy in my DNA, and how Nathan Weiss thought it might prove that I was an alien.

It was all true, yes. But as for being the *whole* truth, it didn't even come close.

For dessert, Mom and Dad served the chocolate truffles they'd been saving for a special occasion. They gushed about how creative I was, and how impressed they were I'd made such a big effort to fit in and how I'd accomplished so much in just the first week of school. I *had* accomplished a lot, I supposed. I'd set up a gambling ring in the cafeteria, and I'd conned Principal Horowitz into keeping it a secret from my parents. But I wasn't sure if that deserved a reward.

Jim kept nudging me under the table. I couldn't blame him.

As soon as we finished clearing the dishes, I hurried to the living room to send Lily an e-mail, just to make sure she was okay. I hadn't heard from her since her aunt Esther had picked her up after school. By the way, you should have seen *her* nose. Aunt Esther's, I mean. It looks like a pig's nose. I know that sounds terrible, and she's not a piglike woman at all. It's just that her nose is wide and flat and the tip turns up, so you can see into her nostrils. Maybe a nicer way of putting it is that she has a "button nose." Except it's the kind of button you'd find on a thick winter overcoat.

Jim followed me into the living room to do his math homework. Mom and Dad headed upstairs. I settled in on the couch across from him and flipped open my laptop.

There was an e-mail waiting for me.

From: manuscriptdecoder@webmail.com
To: samarabrooks@webmail.com
Cc: LilyFrederickprez@mms.edu
Date: September 8
Subject: URGENT!!! PROOF OF ALIENS!!!

Hey, Samara and Lily! You won't believe what I discovered this afternoon! Samara, the molecular configuration really DOES match a pattern in the Voynich Manuscript and Phaistos Disk. Plus you can see it in huge galaxies and tiny microscopic

organisms. IT'S NO COINCIDENCE! Can you
get online??? I want to show it to you!!

"And you think *I* sound like Dr. Frankenstein," I mumbled out loud.

Jim peeked over the top of his calculus textbook. "Can you stop talking to yourself and take your laptop somewhere else? I'm trying to do my homework here."

"Very funny." I knew that if I went upstairs, he would just yell for me to come back down when he got stuck on a problem, which would probably be a lot sooner than later. I hit reply and typed:

From: samarabrooks@webmail.com
To: manuscriptdecoder@webmail.com
Cc: LilyFrederickprez@mms.edu
Date: September 8
Subject: Re: URGENT!!! PROOF OF ALIENS!!!

Hey, Nathan, does this really prove I'm an alien? Kidding. It does sound like an amazing coincidence. But you see coincidences in a lot of things, maybe even more than most people. Like when you play craps, and you roll a seven. You get lucky once, so you think you'll get lucky again. True, the probability is much higher that you'll roll a seven than snake eyes. (One in six as opposed to one in twenty-one.) The problem is, you still have a greater than 80% chance of losing at craps, always. You can look it up. The casino, or "the house" (me) mostly wins. That's why you owe me twelve bucks. I guess what I'm trying to say is that maybe the eye-shaped thingy is just a fluke. Hey, how are you feeling, Lily? Hope you're okay!

I pressed send and leaned back into the cushions.

Jim closed his calculus book and stared at me.

"What?" I said. "I'm not talking to myself. It's totally silent. It's like outer space in here."

"No, I was just thinking . . ."

"Really, you were thinking?" I joked. "Hey, keep it up. You might even like it."

"No, Samara, seriously. Can I ask you something?"

"What?" I said.

"Promise you won't get mad?"

"I'll get mad if you don't tell me what's bugging you."

He squirmed in the sofa cushions. "Did you maybe dream up this experiment to get your hands on your DNA, so you could use it to find out who your real parents are?"

Whoa. I hadn't seen that coming. Finding my real parents had been the farthest notion from my mind. At least, I thought it had.

"I . . . I . . ." I racked my brain for an answer, but none came. Finally I let out a deep breath. "Maybe I just wanted to prove that I really *am* an alien," I mumbled.

"If you want proof, look in the mirror," he cracked lightly, picking up his book.

I hurled a pillow at him. The laptop dinged with a new e-mail: *Beep-beep.*

From: manuscriptdecoder@webmail.com
To: samarabrooks@webmail.com
Cc: LilyFrederickprez@mms.edu
Date: September 8
Subject: Re: Re: URGENT!!! PROOF OF ALIENS!!!

Samara, it's coincidental that you mention probabilities and statistics, because those are a big part of how genes work. So get this. I Googled Dr. Chance. You know, the guy who owned the electron microscope before Madison Middle School did? And you won't believe this. Twenty years ago, he conducted an experiment with his own DNA. I found it online. He posted some photos. He has the same eye pattern in his DNA that you do!!! What is the probability of that??? Look at these jpegs. Then write back ASAP.

The Eye Nebula

Extremophiles

An Excerpt from the Vonyich Manuscript

The Phaistos Disk

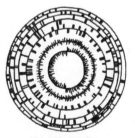

The B. fragilis
NCTC9343 Chromosome

I opened the attachment and took a peek at the five jpegs he sent. I ended up staring for a very long while. I'm not even sure for how long, and usually I'm a pretty good judge of time.

The jpeg of the Cat's Eye Nebula galaxy did look a lot like the jpeg of the so-called extremophiles. And both images looked pretty much exactly like the weird eye pattern we'd seen in my DNA . . . But the drawing from the Voynich Manuscript and the carving in the Phaistos Disk were kind of pushing it. Weren't they?

He didn't include the images from the experiment today, either, because Principal Horowitz and Mrs. Belle hadn't printed the photo negatives. Instead, he included a chart of the "*B. fragilis* NCTC9343 chromosome." That looked *sort* of like what we'd seen, but it didn't have the same genuine eyelike feel. It was more of a cheap knockoff, like those fake watches that real live con artists sell on street corners downtown.

"What's going on?" Jim asked. "Why so freaked out?"

I leaned back and scratched my head. "I don't know. I just got a weird e-mail from Nathan Weiss. He sent me a bunch of pictures that look like that eye-thingy we saw today in my DNA."

Jim tossed his calculus book aside and scooted over beside me, squinting over my shoulder at Nathan's e-mail.

"I don't get it," he said. "How does all this prove you're an alien?"

"I'm not really sure. But who ever knows *what* Nathan's thinking?"

The e-mail dinged again.

From: LilyFrederickprez@mms.edu
To: manuscriptdecoder@webmail.com
Cc: samarabrooks@webmail.com
Date: September 8
Subject: Re: Re: Re: URGENT!!! PROOF OF ALIENS!!!

Hey, Samara and Nathan! I'm really, really sorry I fainted today. Thanks for being so nice and taking care of me, Samara! And thanks for including me in the experiment to get me off the hook for gambling.

Can we meet up tomorrow and talk? You guys can come over to my aunt's if you want. All this stuff about eye patterns and aliens is really neat, but I just got a strange phone call from Detective Rosen. You know, one of the policemen who was with us in the lab today? He told me there was a break-in at school today! Can you believe it? Somebody stole the film negatives from the experiment! He wants to talk to me about it, but he's not allowed to because my parents aren't home and they have to be present if he questions me. Aunt Esther hung up on him, too, because he was rude. Has he called either of you guys yet? Let me know. Thx!

XOXO—Lily

PS: For what it's worth, Samara, I don't think you're an alien!!! ☺

Not Funny "Ha-Ha"

Jim's eyebrows twisted in a furry knot over his nose. "Who would want to steal photo negatives of your DNA?"

"Beats me," I said.

He turned and looked me in the eye. "You didn't do it, did you?"

"Of course not!" I felt a horrible pang of guilt, and I wasn't sure why. It made no sense, and worse, it was bad form. Con artists are never supposed to feel guilty, especially if they're innocent.

"Because I'd understand if you did," Jim said. "You know, if you thought it could help find your real parents."

I wanted to inform him that I'd really appreciate it if he would drop this searching-for-my-real-parents thing for good and shut up every once in a while—but before I could, the phone rang. I hopped off the couch. Maybe I'd gotten lucky. Maybe it was Lily, calling to tell me that the photo strip had been found and the culprit had been caught and we could all forget about the whole thing. But the caller ID showed *Unlisted*.

"Hello?" I answered.

"Yes, hello," a man's gravelly voice replied.

I didn't recognize him. He was tough to hear. There was a rumble in the background on his end. Plus, a car was slowing down in front of our house.

"Is this Samara Brooks?" he asked.

"Who wants to know?" I said, my eyes on Jim.

Jim wasn't paying any attention. He stood and tiptoed over to the window, pushing the curtains aside.

"My name is Detective Frank Rosen," the voice replied. "I'm calling about an incident that occurred at Madison Middle School sometime late this afternoon or early this evening. If Samara Brooks and her parents are available, I'd like to ask her a few questions." The rumble on his end faded to silence, and so did the traffic outside. "Is this Samara Brooks?" he asked again.

Jim turned and beckoned to me, pointing at the glass.

I peered out to the street.

There was a strange car parked at the curb—a big black four-door, like those private taxis Dad takes to the airport when he has to go on business trips. Its lights were on, but its engine was turned off. The streetlamps glittered against its tinted windows.

"Yes, this is Samara Brooks," I said, swallowing. Funny: At the beginning of the week, I'd set out to create some drama. And now that my life was nothing *but* drama, I wished I were invisible again. Maybe it wasn't so funny.

Detective Rosen cleared his throat. "Are your parents home?"

"Yes," I said anxiously. "But do you really need to talk to them?"

"I would like to, if that's all right with you. Detective Gulden is here with me." He paused. "We're right outside."

Impending Doom Isn't a Birthday Bash

My feet wobbled as I marched to the front door. If the police wanted to talk to my parents and me, that was fine, right? I had nothing to hide. Well, not much, anyway. Nothing criminal. But a very unpleasant thought had wormed its way into my head. I'd smothered the electron microscope with my fingerprints. So even though I hadn't stolen the negatives, they would have plenty of evidence to suspect that I had.

Oh well. Might as well get the interrogation over with, I said to myself. Impending doom isn't a birthday bash; there's no fun in the wait. I threw open the door just as they reached the front stoop.

"Good evening," they both greeted me at the same time.

For some reason, Detective Rosen looked a little larger and tubbier than he had earlier that day, but maybe that was because his clothes were baggier. He'd changed into a loose-fitting suit and a tie. His belly oozed out over his belt buckle, stretching his white button-down shirt like an over-stuffed sack of rice.

Detective Gulden had changed into a dark suit, too, only he'd buttoned his jacket. He was definitely the better groomed of the two. He'd even slicked his hair back. In the cold glow of the streetlamps, his thin, pointy nose resembled a narrow slab of white cinderblock, the kind we have in our gym.

"Mind if we come in?" Detective Rosen asked.

"Of course not." I took a step backward and bumped into Jim. "Uh, sorry. This is my brother—"

"Jim," Detective Rosen interrupted. He waddled through the front door. "We met this afternoon. Remember?"

I forced a shrill laugh. "Oh, that's right. I forgot."

Detective Gulden followed him inside and glanced around the living room. "So, your folks are home, correct?"

"They are. One second." I turned toward the stairwell. "Mom? Dad?" I yelled. "Can you come down here for a second? The police are here."

"The police?" came a muffled cry from the second floor.

An instant later, Dad and Mom bounded downstairs.

"What's going on?" Dad asked, out of breath.

Detective Rosen smiled and extended a hand. "Good evening, Mr. Brooks. I'm Detective Rosen, and this is my partner, Detective Gulden."

Dad shook both their hands cautiously. "Pleased to meet you," he said. "I don't understand. Is there a problem?"

"We just wanted to ask your daughter a few questions," Detective Gulden said. "If it's all right with you folks."

Dad nodded, his forehead tightly creased. He stole a puzzled glance at me. Mom stood by the couch, her eyes wide.

"Well, as you may know, your daughter stayed late after school to conduct an experiment today," Detective Rosen said. "One of our colleagues, Dr. Belle, invited us to watch. Samara used the school's special microscope to prove that she doesn't have an evil gene." He smiled suddenly, catching me off guard. "Or something like that. To be honest, we tried to follow along, but it was a little over our heads. Samara, please feel free to interrupt if I get any of the details wrong."

Detective Gulden reached into his suit pocket and pulled out a tiny pad and pencil. "Don't mind me," he said. "I have a lousy memory. I just want to take a few notes so I don't miss anything important."

"The problem is," Detective Rosen said, "we don't have a clear picture of what happened after Samara, Jim, and another student—Lily Frederick—left school. That's why we need all the help we can get."

The room fell silent for a moment.

Something you should know: When you're a con artist, it's pretty easy to tell when other con artists aren't telling the whole truth, either.

what's Illegal and what Isn't

"So, Samara," Detective Gulden began, his pencil poised over his pad. "After you, Lily, and Jim left the science lab, what did you do?"

My mind drew a blank. All I could remember was Jim's charade about being a paramedic. "Um, first we all waited for Lily's aunt. And then Jim drove me home."

"Got it." Detective Rosen raised his eyebrows at Jim. "You have your own car?"

"No—uh, it's my mom's," Jim stammered. For once in his life, he didn't sound supremely cocky. "She takes the bus to work."

"He's a very safe driver," I added lamely.

Detective Gulden began to jot down some notes. "I don't doubt it. Safety is a priority when you're planning to be a doctor, right Jim?"

Oh jeez. I winced.

"Who's planning to be a doctor?" Mom asked.

"I can explain," Jim piped up. His cheeks flushed. "See, this afternoon—"

"Let's just stick to what happened after you left school," Detective Rosen interrupted. He winked at Jim. "So you didn't return to the science lab for any reason? Either of you? You know, to pick up something you might have forgotten? The results of your experiment, maybe?"

Both Jim and I shook our heads.

"So what did you do?" Detective Rosen asked.

"W-we came straight home," I stuttered. "And we've been here ever since. I spent the rest of the afternoon on Blackjack.com—" *Ugh.* I shut my mouth. I could feel Mom's and Dad's eyes bearing down on me. "What I mean to say is, I wasn't doing anything wrong," I finished.

Both policemen burst into laughter.

Detective Rosen began to cough, his face beet red. He shoved his fist against his mouth. I watched him worriedly. I'd already seen one person faint today. I didn't really feel like seeing another.

"I'm sorry, Mr. and Mrs. Brooks," Detective Gulden said. "But you should know, your daughter is too young to be gambling online. That *is* illegal."

"I'll make sure it doesn't happen again," my mom promised. Her tone was sharp. She glared at me. "You can be certain of that."

"Don't worry," Detective Rosen choked out. He sounded as if he were snoring, even though he was awake. "We don't plan on . . . slapping the cuffs on your daughter . . . and hauling her down to the station."

"Hey, are you all right?" I asked.

"Fine, fine." He hacked one last time. "Thanks for asking. You can be very polite when you want to be, Samara."

"Thanks." I turned and smiled hopefully at my parents. They didn't smile back.

Normal color slowly returned to his cheeks. "Anyway, while you were here at home, the rest of us had a very interesting chat in the library," Detective Rosen continued. "It lasted until well past five o'clock."

"Who's the rest of you?" Dad wanted to know.

"Samara's classmate, Nathan Weiss, for one," Detective Gulden said, scribbling away. "Kind of a funny kid. He kept saying that you discovered proof of aliens. Even our colleague's wife was impressed. She kept talking about something called intelligent design." He grinned at his partner, then turned back to me. "Now, we don't know about any of this. It's not our business. Our business is the destruction of school property and these missing photo negatives. So are you going to help us or not, Samara?"

Wasted Truffles

Once again, silence fell over the room. Part of me wished that they *would* haul me down to the police station. At least then I wouldn't have to face Mom and Dad when this was all over. Finally I mustered the courage to speak up.

"I swear to you, I'm just as surprised as you are about all this," I said. "I don't even know what happened exactly."

"Yeah, Lily Frederick told us the same thing word for word," Detective Rosen answered casually. "She claims that she doesn't know what happened, either. But I kind of had the feeling that she was covering for somebody."

"Who?" I croaked, even though I knew the answer.

"Not really sure. She's kind of a funny kid, too. I'm not

sure how it came up, but she also mentioned that you once told her you wouldn't break her legs."

"She said that?" I cried, aghast. "When?"

"On the phone, about an hour ago. Relax, relax," Detective Rosen soothed. "We just had a chat, Lily and I. And her aunt Esther."

"What did you talk about?"

"Well, mostly about what *we* know," he said. "That shortly after we all left Madison Middle School this afternoon, somebody ransacked the science lab and stole a strip of photo negatives from the electron microscope." He stared at me. "We wondered what kind of a person would do such a thing."

My stomach squeezed.

"I think that might have been when Lily mentioned that you wouldn't break her legs," Detective Gulden put in.

"Right! I wouldn't break her legs! I'm not a—" I paused, my pulse racing. "I'm not . . . a . . . you know . . ."

"No, we don't know," Detective Rosen said. "Tell us."

"I'm not somebody who would break a person's legs," I finished, avoiding my family's flabbergasted stares. "Not even close."

"What's close?" Detective Gulden asked. "Running a casino out of your school cafeteria and shaking your class president down for sixty-three big ones?"

Blood drained from my face. *Well, Mom and Dad, I bet you're probably wishing you hadn't wasted those chocolate truffles on me tonight.*

Detective Rosen clucked his tongue. "Samara, I don't mean to alarm your parents. But who's not to say that by telling Lily you wouldn't break her legs, you were showing her that you maybe could? That it was a slight threat, even if it wasn't all that serious?"

"No, no, no. You don't get it. I *stink* at showing. I *only* tell. You can ask my English teacher. I'd never threaten Lily. I'd never threaten anyone!"

"Why's that?" Detective Gulden asked matter-of-factly, scribbling once more on his notepad. "What if someone deserved it?"

"But Lily and I are friends!"

"Friends?" He seemed dubious. "Interesting."

I froze. "What? Why is that interesting? Did Lily say something?"

"That's between you two. But I *would* like you and Lily to be friends, Samara. I'd like you to be friends with Nathan Weiss, too. I'd like for us all to be friends. Because friends cooperate. And the sooner we all cooperate, the sooner this little mystery gets solved and we can all get on with our lives. Am I right?"

122

I nodded, unable to breathe.

"So you're absolutely sure that there's nothing you want to tell us?" Detective Rosen asked. "You're absolutely sure you had nothing to do with breaking into your school's science lab and stealing something that doesn't belong to you?"

"Of course not!" I cried.

"Okay," Detective Gulden said. "If you say so." He snapped his notepad shut.

"Well, I think that about does it for this evening," Detective Rosen said after a moment. "If you can think of anything you might want to tell us, or any detail that might have slipped your mind, just give us a call." He reached into his rumpled jacket pocket and handed Dad a small white card. "Here's my contact info. You can call me anytime, twenty-four-seven."

"It was a pleasure to meet you folks," Detective Gulden said. "We'll be in touch."

Mom and Dad nodded as the detectives sauntered out the door, whispering to each other on the front walk. Detective Gulden turned when he reached the car.

"You know, I could understand why a smart kid like you would want those negatives, Samara," he said. "Now, I don't think you have an evil gene or anything like that. But you are a gambler. A risk-taker. I bet you saw dollar signs." He made quotes in the air with his fingers. "'The heartwarming story of how an eighth grader discovered proof of aliens.' Ha! Hey, I'd swipe 'em myself. That's the kind of thing that can make you famous." He glanced over the car at his partner. "Right?"

He and Detective Rosen exchanged a laugh.

I tried to gulp, but my throat was too parched.

"Thanks again for your cooperation," Detective Gulden called.

Time slowed to a painful crawl as they climbed into the car and pulled away from the curb. I watched their taillights disappear down the block. Even when the sound of the engine had faded into the night and the street was deserted and all I heard were crickets, I still couldn't move. I could have stood there all night until the sun rose. Anything to avoid turning around and facing my family.

The Trouble Between My Mouth and My Brain

The phone rang.

"Got it!" I squeaked. I whirled and dashed past my parents, grabbing the phone off the side table, then flew up the stairwell, taking three steps at a time.

"Samara!" Mom yelled.

"Hello?" I answered without even bothering to check the caller ID.

"Hello? Samara? It's Lily."

"Lily?" I gasped. I slammed my bedroom door and locked it, then collapsed on my bed in the darkness. "Wow, am I glad to hear from you—"

"What's going on?" she interrupted. "Are you okay?"

"Not really. The cops were just here." I held my breath. "Are *you* okay?"

She let out a sad little laugh. "I've had better days, I guess. Listen, I'm on the other line with Nathan right now. Aunt Esther showed me how to dial a three-way call. I can conference you in."

Conference me in? I wondered. It sounded like something my dad would say. I stared up at the dark ceiling. Was Lily mad at me? Maybe she really *did* think I had an evil gene or that I'd break her legs. It was my fault she'd gotten mixed up in all this insanity to begin with. I felt sick to my stomach.

The phone clicked. "Samara? Are you there? I think I have Nathan on the line. . . ."

"I'm here, Lily," Nathan said.

"I'm here, too," I croaked.

"I'm here, three," Lily said. She tried to laugh again. "Sorry, dumb joke."

"Hey, Samara, did you look at those jpegs I sent?" Nathan asked. "You see what I mean about how all the images look exactly the same—"

"Wait, wait, Nathan," Lily interrupted. "I'm sorry. But Samara, are *you* okay? I'm worried about you."

My brow furrowed. "You are?"

My doorknob shook. "Samara?" Dad called. He pounded on the door. "Can you open up, please? Your mother and I would like a word with you."

I squeezed my eyes shut. *Why can't I just be invisible again?* I wondered. But there was no point in complaining, even to myself. I'd set out to create some drama, and I'd gotten it—in spades. Mission accomplished.

"Samara!" Dad barked.

"Hey, Dad, can you just give me two minutes?" I begged, covering the mouthpiece with my hand. "Please? I really need to talk to Lily and Nathan right now. I know it's not really fair to ask . . . but I swear, as soon as I'm done talking with them I'll come out and explain everything."

"Fine," Dad said. "But when you do, you'd better have what you took from school today."

"But I didn't take anything!" I cried. I sat up and feverishly ran a hand through my hair, then clamped it down on the mouthpiece again. "Two minutes, all right? Just give me two minutes. Please."

"*One* minute," Dad countered. He stormed back down the hall.

I cradled the phone against my cheek, my fingers trembling. "Sorry," I whispered. "Lily? Nathan? You guys still there?"

"Still here," they both answered at the same time.

"Okay, listen. I don't have much time to talk. But Lily, you're right about what you said in your e-mail—we should definitely meet up at your aunt Esther's tomorrow. Is that still on?"

"Sure, of course," Lily said.

"I might have a hard time getting out of the house," Nathan muttered. "My mom thinks I stole the photo negatives from the science lab because I want to prove to the world that I've been right all along about aliens."

If I hadn't been so frightened and miserable, I would have laughed. For once I could relate to him. "My parents think I stole the negatives, too," I said. "So do the police. Which is why we have to figure out who really *did* do it."

"Who do you think?" Lily asked.

I shook my head. "I don't know. But whoever did it did a really good job of pinning it on me."

"Me too," Nathan added.

"Me three," Lily murmured.

"Right." I drew in a deep breath. "So that's why we have to figure this thing out. As soon as possible, before we get into any more trouble. How early can we meet?"

"I say the crack of dawn," Nathan answered before Lily could respond. "If we have to sneak out of our houses—and I know I will—we should meet outside your aunt's house right before the sun comes up."

"I think you're right," I said. "Lily, is that cool?"

"Yeah." She didn't sound so sure.

Angry footsteps pounded back toward my door. "Samara!" Dad shouted. "One minute is up! Your mother and I want you out here *now*!"

"I'll e-mail you guys my aunt's address tonight," Lily said quickly. "It's about a ten-minute bike ride from school. So if we all have bikes . . ."

"I do," Nathan said. "Look, I better go. See you tomorrow."

There was a click.

"Samara?" Lily said. "You still there?"

"Yeah. I've got to go, too, though. But listen, Lily, are we friends? You know, like, *really*?" I couldn't believe I'd just asked that. I definitely hadn't *wanted* to ask that. During the past week, my mouth had developed a very annoying habit of operating separately from my brain. Not good for a con artist.

"Of course we're friends, Samara," Lily said as if that were the silliest question in the world. "Why do you even ask?"

"Because the cops acted like *you* said we weren't friends. You know, because I threatened you and all that."

She chuckled softly. "And you believed them? You run a gambling ring, Samara."

"I guess you have a point."

"I'll see you tomorrow, okay?" she said. "We'll figure this thing out."

I hung up. A strange knot had formed in my throat. My eyes stung, too, but for some ridiculous reason, I started to smile. And as I pushed myself to my feet and plodded toward the door, I realized that I wasn't even all that scared of facing Mom and Dad. I have no idea why. My brain was on the fritz. No wonder my mouth had decided to cut loose of it these past few days. Because all I could think was *We've managed to count to two together, Lily and I.*

129

Part Five
NATHAN WEISS

SNEAKING OUT OF my house Saturday morning was easier than I thought. My mom snores, so that helped. I tiptoed down to the garage and, as quietly as I could, lifted the door about waist high. Then I crouched under and dragged my bike out with a grunt. I didn't bother to close the door behind me.

This is a terrible, terrible idea, I thought. But I hopped on my bike anyway.

I pedaled down the street as fast as I could. I'd hoped the damp predawn air might perk me up a little, but it didn't. It was barely five o'clock, too early for the joggers and dog-walkers, even, and the sky was a deep, deep blue—dark enough to see the brightest stars. The stillness of the neighborhood made me feel weirdly lonely somehow, as if I were the only person alive on the planet.

I thought about the last time I'd snuck out on my mom. It was the only other time I'd ever snuck out in my life.

Something you should know about my mom: *She* was the one who planted the idea in my head that God was an alien. She didn't mean to, but it happened during one of the biggest fights she and Dad had at the end of their marriage nearly a year ago. And it happened, of all days, on Yom Kippur: the day you're supposed to skip every meal and tell God how sorry you are for all the lousy things you've done.

We were sitting at the breakfast table. Dad was smoothing the wrinkles in his suit, glaring at Mom. Mom was still in her pajamas, chewing a bagel, slurping coffee, and reading a book called *The Bible Code.*

DAD: Helen, you know you're supposed to be fasting right now.

MOM: Oh, relax, David. Have you looked at this book? I mean, really?

DAD: Forget the book. I'm talking about having breakfast on Yom Kippur.

MOM: Hey, as long as I believe in God, it doesn't matter what I do.

DAD: You're setting a terrible example for Nathan. I'm leaving.

MOM: Okay. Have fun. Say hi to Rabbi Levy for me. He's a riot.

DAD: Listen to you! Yom Kippur is not about having fun or being a riot!

MOM (shrugging and sipping coffee): Who says?

DAD (veins bulging and about to burst): God says!

MOM: How do you know? Did you and God have a chat? Maybe God has a better sense of humor than you think. You should read this book, David. You'll

133

believe in God more than ever before. You just think about him the wrong way. He's an alien. He's alien to us because he's so much smarter. He sees the entire future. He encoded it in the Torah! Did you know that people who've figured out the code can use it to predict actual events?[4]

DAD: Good-bye, Helen. Have fun with your Bible Code. I hope God sees fit to forgive you.

That was when I snuck out.

I ended up riding my bike around aimlessly for a few hours. Mom never did make me go to temple later, even though it was the most important holiday of the year, *and* my bar mitzvah was less than four months away. But I didn't care. I even thought about quitting Hebrew school for good.

See, the God I learned about during that fight was the one who began to make sense to me, way more than the God I had to study at Hebrew school. Because math isn't like life. It isn't like parents, or any other kind of crap a person has to

---

[4] The theory of *The Bible Code* is that God actually wrote the Torah. He encoded everything about everyone in the text, too—and I mean *everything,* throughout all history—which means everything about you and me. To put it another way, if I wanted to find out who stole the negatives, I could actually look it up in the Torah. I would just have to know the code. Too bad I didn't.

deal with. Math never changes. It can't. It's sort of perfect that way.

Samara and Lily were already waiting with their bikes outside Lily's aunt's house by the time I skidded up to the curb. They looked as if they'd rolled right out of bed and straight into two rumpled, oversized sweaters. They were also wearing matching green bike helmets. They could have been twins.

"Did you two coordinate your outfits?" I asked, trying to lighten the mood. It didn't go over so well.

"Coincidence, Nathan," Samara said dryly. "Another random coincidence, given all our outfit probabilities. But thanks for pointing it out. Still think I'm an alien?"

"No, not really," I mumbled. "Sorry."

Lily glanced across the lawn toward her aunt's darkened windows. "We should probably keep our voices down," she whispered. "I don't want to wake up Aunt Esther. Did you know that the break-in is already in the news?"

"It is?" Samara and I gasped at the same time.

Lily nodded anxiously. "I read the *Madison Tribune* online when I woke up. It was on the front page of the local section. 'Theft and Vandalism at Madison Middle School.' That was the headline."

I swallowed. "Did it say anything about the police?"

She nodded. "It said that they were investigating. It didn't mention any of us by name, just that a 'group of students' stayed late after school to conduct an experiment with a 'rare and expensive microscope.' Those were the words."

"Look, maybe we should just get going," Samara said. She hopped on her bike. "If my parents wake up and come looking for me, I'm dead. No exaggeration."

"Where to?" Lily asked.

"I had an idea last night," Samara said, weaving in small circles. "I'll explain it on the way. It'll take us about an hour or so to get there, at least. Follow me."

I stood there clutching my handlebars, watching Lily follow Samara with a wobbly start. *An hour or so?* I probably should have snagged a little snack to go on my way out. Maybe we could make a pit stop. Of course, I didn't have any money.

"Wait up!" I jumped on and pedaled after them.

"So here's what I'm thinking," Samara called over her shoulder. Luckily, the street sloped downward for a few blocks, so we could coast for a bit and concentrate on our plan—if we even had one. "Whoever stole those negatives had to know how to use the electron microscope, right? Or at least, they had to be familiar enough with it to be able to get the negatives *out* of it, is what I'm saying."

I nodded. "Yeah, you're right. When we all left the library yesterday, Mrs. Belle said she was going to wait until Monday to print the negatives. I guess the whole process is sort of a hassle. She said it takes, like, fifteen minutes, and she and Dr. Belle wanted to go home."

"You don't think . . . ," Lily began.

"Mrs. Belle stole them?" Samara finished. "You know, I did wonder about that. What if she hates her job? And she was looking for a way to quit? Maybe she made it look like the point of the crime was to steal the negatives—but the real point was to ransack the science lab. The negatives were just a red herring."

"A what?" Lily asked.

"A decoy," Samara said.

I blinked in the onrushing wind. "No way. That's nuts. I mean—no offense, Samara—but I know Mrs. Belle pretty well. She *loves* being a science teacher. She's always the first to get to school and the last to leave. She's even more of a geek than I am."

Lily laughed. "You're not a geek, Nathan."

"That's nice of you, Lily, but the election was over last spring," Samara teased. "You already have Nathan's vote."

I would have teased Samara back, but an unpleasant thought began to prickle in the back of my mind. What if

Samara was right? What if Mrs. Belle *did* hate being a science teacher? Maybe she was just really good at pretending she loved it. And maybe—just maybe—she'd been trying to send that message to someone, to anyone. Even me. Could that be what her riddle, Skipping on All Fours, was meant to do?

Fill in ten big dots. Tip the stew. Tuck in open drapes. Do not powwow.

I slowed to a stop at the bottom of the hill. My heart jumped. And in that instant, without the slightest bit of concentration—without even *trying*—the solution to the riddle clicked into place, as if a timer had gone off inside my head *(Ding!)*. The gears in my brain fired up and meshed perfectly together.

"I've solved it!" I said out loud.

"Solved what?" Lily asked. She and Samara pulled up beside me.

"Mrs. Belle's riddle." I grinned, my breath coming fast. "I've figured it out."

"What is it?" Samara said.

"Find the code now," I proclaimed.[5]

The girls kept looking at me, baffled.

---

[5] FILLINTENBIGDOTSTIPTHESTEWTUCKINOPENDRAPESDONOTPOWWOW

"What does that mean?" Lily asked.

"It doesn't mean anything, really," I said. "It's just a little brainteaser. Words inside of gibberish. That's why the title is so nonsensical. Skipping on All Fours. It's meant for someone who tries to find codes hidden in *everything*. Like me, I guess."

Samara's lips curled in a smile. "I see now," she said. "Skipping on All Fours. All four *letters*. And that's what Mrs. Belle meant by 'Only one out of four counts if you're trying to make sense.' One out of four letters. *That's* the code."

"Exactly," I said.

"I'm sorry," Lily apologized. "I'm still confused."

"Don't worry," Samara said. "It *is* a little confusing. But now that we've cracked it . . . I don't know. I'd have a really hard time believing Mrs. Belle could possibly ransack the science lab and steal the negatives. She *is* a geek. In a good way, I mean. She's exactly what she seems. There's nothing hidden."

I nodded, feeling very relieved. "Right."

Lily struggled not to yawn. "So now that we've ruled out Mrs. Belle, what's next? Where are you taking us, Samara?"

Samara pointed through the intersection, over the rooftops and toward the hills at the edge of town. The sun was just poking over the horizon.

"We're going up there," she said. "We're going to pay Dr. Chance a visit."

"The guy who owned the microscope?" I asked. "When I Googled him, it said he moved someplace far away."

"He did. But I was surfing the Web, too, going crazy trying to figure this whole thing out, and I discovered that he moved back just last year. He's retired now."

Lily rubbed her bleary eyes. "Wait— Why are we going to visit him?"

"Because if anyone knows how to swipe film negatives from Madison Middle School's fabulous electron microscope," Samara replied, "it's Dr. Chance."

A long, long time ago—before I was born, even—back when my parents were rumored to get along, they used to spend weekend getaways together at a campground called Whispering Oaks.

Coincidentally, Whispering Oaks happened to be the exact same spot where Dr. Chance had chosen to settle down and retire.

I'd seen pictures in Mom's photo album: a rustic clump of cabins perched high in the hills. (*Way* too high up for bicycles.) She and Dad would practice yoga, cook their meals over an open fire, and swim in a freshwater stream. They even took me there once, but I was so young that all I remember is the color of the trees. It was fall, and at sunrise, the whole world turned a blinding orange. In my memory—or at least, the way my childish brain had once worked—it seemed as if the hills were on fire.

The oaks were green now, but at sunrise they were still tinted with that same fiery orange glow. The campground wasn't much to look at anymore, though. It had practically turned into a trailer park. There were still cabins, but parked among the trees were an equal number of trailers—rusting and shabbily painted, with filthy windows.

I didn't get it. *This* was where Dr. Chance wanted to spend the rest of his life?

Then again, the whole place could have just rubbed me the wrong way because my mood had turned from sour to crappy to worse. Biking up here wasn't just stupid; it was insane. I'm pretty sure none of us had ever ridden so far, up such a steep road, for so long, ever. I know I hadn't. (Who *would*, other than an Olympic athlete?) By the time we pedaled up to the two massive oaks that marked the campground entrance, my thighs had stiffened so much that I couldn't keep my balance.

The three of us collapsed from our bikes one by one. We tore off our helmets and sat on our rumps in the packed dirt at the head of the path, our chests heaving.

"What time is it?" Lily groaned hoarsely.

Samara wiped her forehead and peeked at her watch. "A little past seven o'clock."

My stomach rumbled. The campground smelled of old fires, with a whiff of something delicious for dinner the night before.

"Is anybody else as thirsty as I am?" Lily asked.

"There's a stream close by," I said. "You can drink from it."

"I really hope Dr. Chance is home," Samara mumbled. "Mostly because I want to ask him if he can make us breakfast."

I glanced around, shielding my eyes from the sun with my hand. "Do you know which one of these trailers is his?"

She shook her head. "The link I found on the Internet just said he lived here. It didn't give an address or anything."

"Perfect," I grumbled. I staggered to my feet. My legs and ankles burned.

"Hey, don't get mad at me," Samara huffed. "I'm just trying to solve the crime that the cops are trying to pin on *us*. If it were up to you, you'd still be at home trying to prove that I'm an alien."

I scowled at her, sweat dripping from my nose. "I don't really think you're an alien, Samara. I just think that there's something weird in your DNA. And I'm not the only one. Dr. and Mrs. Belle thought so, too. It's a big deal. So maybe it would have been a better idea to figure out exactly *what* was on those negatives first, which would help us figure out *why* somebody would want to steal them—instead of pedaling up to the boondocks on a wild-goose chase."

"Just think how easy the ride home will be," Samara shot back.

"Oh, brother," I moaned. "Can you for once in your life stop being a comedian?"

"Don't fight, you guys," Lily pleaded. "We're all just tired and thirsty and grumpy. And I don't know about you, but I'm freaked out." She sighed. "I'm sorry. I wanted to say . . . You know, I feel like this whole thing is my fault."

I turned to her. "How could this be *your* fault? *You* didn't do anything."

"Yeah, I did. I got hooked on gambling." She kicked at the dirt. "And if I hadn't, then Samara wouldn't have made up that experiment, and nobody would have stolen those negatives, and we wouldn't be out here in the middle of nowhere."

"Um, Lily?" Samara said softly. "That doesn't make any sense at all."

For once, I agreed with her. I chewed my parched lips. "Look, I'm going to try to hunt down this stream. You guys can rest here. I'll holler if I find it."

Samara stood. "I'll come with you."

Lily dragged herself up behind her. "Wait! Don't leave me."

The three of us ambled down the path, threading our way through the silent trailers and cabins. Aside from a few birds and the occasional buzzing mosquito, the place was dead. No voices. No sign of Dr. Chance. I strained my ears, listening for the stream. Nothing. We paused when we reached the edge of the clearing, where the path turned to a trail that disappeared into a thick, shadowy tangle of trees.

"Can I ask you guys something?" Samara said.

"You want to turn around and go home?" I suggested.

"No." Her head drooped. "It's just . . . um . . . you don't really think I have an evil gene, do you?"

I almost laughed. "Where did that come from?"

She jammed her hands in her pockets, avoiding my eyes. "I don't know. It's just what you said a second ago. About how Dr. and Mrs. Belle thought that eye-thingy was such a big deal. Maybe it means . . . you know, I really *am* different."

"Samara, I think the bike ride turned your brain mushy," Lily said. "There's no *way* you have an evil gene."

"How do you know?" she said.

"Because you're the only casino operator on the planet who doesn't collect from the people who lose!" Lily cried. "We might as well have played for Monopoly money."

Samara smiled faintly. "Thanks. I guess."

"And you want to know something else?" Lily said. "If you do have an evil gene, then I have one, too. Because for what it's worth, I don't really think it's so bad that the science lab was ransacked. And if the thieves damaged the electron microscope, too, fine. Maybe Principal Horowitz will finally get rid of it for good. It was ugly, and it took up way too much room. Besides, it caused nothing but trouble."

A strange thought popped into my head. "Hey, what if Principal Horowitz really *did* want to get rid of it?" I said.

Lily and Samara turned to me. "What do you mean?"

"He was acting really weird yesterday morning, remember?" I said. "All jumpy?"

Samara knit her eyebrows. "Yeah? So?"

"Well, you mentioned he was getting a divorce, right?" I said. "Maybe he staged the whole theft to get the microscope out of the lab. I bet he plans to sell it on eBay or something because he's really in a pinch. I know when my parents got divorced, all they talked about was how they were going broke paying for their lawyers."

Neither Samara nor Lily answered. They'd tuned out altogether, their eyes glued to something behind me on the path. I spun around—and nearly jumped.

Standing before me was a stooped, watery-eyed old man with a bushy white beard and crinkly skin the color of sand. His jowls sagged, tugging the corners of his lips down with them. A dented metal canteen hung from his neck. He wore hiking boots and a loose-fitting blue raincoat with stitching above the breast pocket: *Dr. Archibald Chance, MD, PhD.*

"Care for some water?" he offered.

It's never wise to accept a drink from a stranger, I realize. It's one of those don'ts that ranks up there with "Don't play with matches" or "Don't leave the door unlocked." But when the morning sun is bearing down on you and your aching legs are melting beneath the weight of your body and your throat is turning to dried putty . . . you tend to forget about what's wise and what isn't.

I glanced at Samara. As usual, she shrugged.

Lily forced an unhappy smile.

"Um, thanks," I said.

"Yes, thanks," Samara said. She stepped forward.

I watched nervously as Dr. Chance handed her the canteen. His gnarled fingers trembled. Samara tilted her head back and chugged for several seconds, water trickling down her chin. I was half expecting her to turn purple or drop right into the dirt. But when she finished she took a deep breath and smiled.

"Ahh." She handed the canteen to Lily. "Go ahead. It's ice cold."

Lily's fingers trembled even more than Dr. Chance's. But she bravely lifted the canteen to her lips and belted down a mouthful. Then she smiled, too.

"Here you go, Nathan." She passed the canteen to me.

Normally, I'm the type of person who hates sipping from somebody else's glass. Then again, normally, I'm the type of person who doesn't sneak out at dawn to bike up a mountain. I gulped down the water so quickly that I nearly choked. "Thanks," I said, gasping. Cool relief flowed down through my gullet, pooling in the pit of my stomach.

"So what brings you three kids up here so early on a Saturday?" Dr. Chance asked. He plucked the canteen from my hands and draped it back around his neck.

Lily and I both turned to Samara.

"Well, ah . . . we were looking for you, actually," Samara said, matching Lily's frozen smile. "I'm not sure where to begin. This is going to sound a little crazy, but we're students at Madison Middle School."

His eyes twinkled. "What's so crazy about that?"

"No, no—that's not the crazy part." Samara laughed. "What

I meant to say is, we go to the school where your electron microscope ended up. You know, the one you donated to the Madison Police Department years and years ago?"

He tilted his head and peered at her curiously, stroking his beard. "You don't say." He chuckled. "My goodness. I haven't thought about *that* in ages. How did the microscope ever end up at your school?"

"It's sort of a long story," she said.

"By the way, I had a very good reason for handing that microscope over to the police," he whispered conspiratorially. "I wanted to draw attention to a certain fraud of a preacher who cost me my old job."

"Dr. Willis, right?" Samara asked.

Lily stiffened, staring at him. "Wait, *you* know Dr. Willis?"

"I wouldn't call him a doctor, by any means, but yes." Dr. Chance's tone hardened. "The man is nothing more than a crook. A con artist."

"You really think so?" Lily's cheeks turned pinkish. "Why?"

"Because he preys upon the weak!" His voice rose. "And he claims to do the opposite! And the lies he tells! He's a criminal of the worst kind. All this nonsense about how the Bible should be taken at face value, word for word, and how human beings and dinosaurs all lived together at the same time, and—" He broke off. "You'll have to excuse me. My blood boils when I think about it."

Lily began to wring her hands. "Maybe he's just trying to show people that there are hidden messages in the Bible," she said, sounding distressed. "Maybe that's what he means by taking it word for word."

I frowned at her. "What's the matter? Do you know Dr. Willis, too?"

"Well, not personally," she muttered. "He's the preacher at the church Aunt Esther belongs to. We listen to his radio show whenever she drives me to school."

"Please don't tell me he's hoodwinked you, young lady," Dr. Chance said gravely. "Please don't tell me you believe his lies."

Lily lifted her shoulders. "I—"

"Hey, listen, we don't really have to talk about Dr. Willis," Samara cut in. "We're all just a little hung up on hidden messages because of this experiment we conducted with your old microscope."

"Is that so?" Dr. Chance raised his eyebrows.

"Yeah. See, we examined a strand of my hair, to see what my DNA looks like, and there was this funny eye-shaped thingy in it," Samara explained.

"And it fit a pattern," I added. "So that got all of us started on different theories. My science teacher and her husband thought it could be proof of something called intelligent design. But *I* thought it could be proof of something alien. Because it looked exactly like these microscopic bugs called extremophiles, and huge galaxies, and images in this ancient book called the Voynich Manuscript, and an even more ancient old plate called the Phaistos Disk . . ." All of a sudden, I regretted opening my mouth. I realized that I sounded like a complete nutcase.

Dr. Chance's face brightened.

"What is it?" Lily asked.

"This is the most extraordinary coincidence!" he exclaimed.

Samara glanced at Lily and me. "It is?"

He shuffled down the narrow path that sliced into the forest. "Follow me," he said excitedly. "I want to show you my video on the theory of the universal mind!"

If accepting a drink from a stranger is unwise, then accepting a stranger's invitation to see a video on the theory of something called the universal mind would clearly qualify as idiotic. I'm sure Samara and Lily thought so, anyway. An old man living alone on a mountaintop, jabbering incomprehensibly and disappearing off into the wilderness—aka ingredients for a slasher film—would not put a nice, normal, sane person at ease. But the amazing (or pathetic) truth, depending on your point of view, was that I knew exactly what he was talking about.

"Uh, Nathan?" Samara said. "Can you wait up a sec?"

"It's okay, I promise," I called over my shoulder. "Come on."

Her face soured, but she trotted after me, tugging Lily along with her.

Once on the trail, the air grew still and quiet. Our footsteps crunched on the earth. Overhead, the leaves and branches shimmered like one big emerald green curtain, shielding us from the sun. Dr. Chance deftly skirted an occasional fallen tree trunk, leading us farther and farther from the campground. Alarm bells should have been blasting in my brain, but they weren't. Of all the coincidences we'd encountered in the past twenty-four hours, *this* was the wildest.

I probably should have explained why to Samara and Lily. But I figured Dr. Chance could do a better job. He was the professor, after all.

Here's the thing. Not long after Mom accidentally sparked my curiosity about aliens, I'd stumbled upon a blog: www.theoryoftheuniversalmind.org. It was written by a bunch of eccentric scientists who devoted all their spare time to searching for proof of extraterrestrial intelligence.

Anybody else—Samara or Lily, or all the other kids I

knew—would have lumped the blog right in with phony psychic hotlines or "true tales from beyond the grave" or other nonsense and never clicked on it again. But to me, it read like a detective novel. It zigzagged from outer space to archaeological digs to stories of raining frogs (seriously), and every single entry triggered an idea in the next—like a row of tumbling dominoes.

One theorized that the Egyptian pyramids were control towers for UFOs. That in turn got someone started on the Nazca Lines, huge drawings in the deserts of Peru, which from ground level look like dead-end roads but from high altitudes look like birds or even landing strips. And *that* led to a discussion of Stonehenge, and how it could be a big traffic sign for spacecraft. . . . And now that I thought about it, the blog was less like a row of dominoes and more like a single thread woven into a magical, impossible tapestry.

Jeez. Magical, impossible tapestry? I should definitely leave the talking to Dr. Chance. I could just picture how I'd sound to Samara and Lily.

The path grew brighter ahead. After a few more twists in the trail, we emerged in a weed-choked meadow. A lone farmhouse sat at the far edge, its peeling white paint glistening in the sunshine, a rickety porch swing swaying in the breeze. Tendrils of smoke drifted from the stone chimney.

"That's my home," Dr. Chance announced proudly. "Or one of them, anyway. I built it myself years and years ago, with a little help from some friends."

Samara sniffed the air. "Do I smell bacon?"

My mouth watered.

"Breakfast ham," Dr. Chance replied. "There's plenty if you're hungry."

"Oh, I'm fine," Samara lied smoothly. "Thanks, though."

Dr. Chance gingerly picked his way through the tall grass. "Ever wonder why bacon or ham smells so delicious?" he asked of nobody in particular. "Because a long, long time ago, before human beings fully evolved, we had to rely on our noses for survival. Our noses were the first line of defense against poison, or any other kind of danger. But thanks to the universal mind, we can use our brains. Our noses aren't chimps' noses. Now we can enjoy smells for the pleasure of them."

Hmm. I cringed. Maybe I *should* try to help clarify a few things. I'd do my best to sound reasonable.

"See, what he means is that millions of years ago, aliens helped chimps turn into human beings," I told Samara and Lily. "That's what people mean when they talk about the missing link. That's part of the theory of the universal mind."

Samara and Lily dithered behind us in the meadow. Their

noses wrinkled, as if the breakfast ham had turned to rotten compost.

"Is that true, Dr. Chance?" Samara asked.

"It is, it is," he replied, climbing the porch steps. They creaked beneath his boots. He paused at the front door and grinned impishly. "Well, before I invite you into my home, I should probably learn your names, shouldn't I?"

"I'm Nathan Weiss," I said. I scampered up to shake his hand.

He took it and let go quickly, peering at Samara and Lily. They hesitated at the bottom of the steps.

"Samara and Lily," Samara reluctantly answered for the both of them.

Dr. Chance arched an eyebrow. "No last names?"

"I think they're a little shy," I whispered to him. "Neither of them knows about the theory of the universal mind. They're probably confused."

"Oh, I see. Perfectly understandable. Now, who's who?"

"I'm Samara." She nudged Lily, who bit her lip.

Dr. Chance opened the door and held it for me. "Well, it's a pleasure to meet all three of you, Nathan, Samara, and Lily."

The girls didn't budge.

"If you're upset about what I said about your preacher

friend, I apologize, Lily," Dr. Chance said. "I take it you're a very religious young lady?"

"I guess so," she said, sounding sheepish.

"I am too, in a way." He stroked his beard thoughtfully. "Jesus, or God, is just another name for the universal mind. Jesus told the people of the world to be nice to each other. He said, 'Love everyone else as you love yourself.' And I certainly concur. Because imagine what God thought of us before we evolved? He saw a bunch of hairy apes beating each other with clubs all those eons ago. And he thought, 'Enough! Stop the fighting! Use your brains instead!' So Jesus—or even others like him—planted a little something of himself inside them. Which is how we humans came to be."

I couldn't tell if Lily was being polite, or if she was creeped out or miffed over his blather to trust herself to speak—but she didn't utter a peep of protest. She hiked up the stairs, with Samara right behind her. I almost felt like thanking her. I could only imagine what was going through her mind.

Dr. Chance closed the door.

The curtains were drawn. The scent of ham was stronger inside, but the air was stale and musty. Hundreds of books lined the walls: mostly thick leather-bound volumes, and a few crumbling paperbacks. What with the Persian rug and the parlor lamps and the bulky computer perched on the scarred mahogany desk, it looked as if this place had been frozen in time at least twenty years ago, if not more.

"Have a seat if you like," Dr. Chance said. He motioned toward a sofa strewn with some frayed throw pillows.

Well. If Dr. Chance turned out to be some sort of demented serial killer, there was no way I could run for it now. I was too exhausted. I sank into the upholstery, grimacing. Samara and Lily flopped down on either side of me.

Dr. Chance puttered over to the desk and flipped on his computer. "It's nice to have company so young and smart," he said. I wondered if he was trying to put us at ease. "And I want to help you girls understand where I'm coming from so you don't write me off as some old kook. Because your friend Nathan reminds me of friends I had in the past, back when I was a student at MIT. We used to stay up into the wee hours talking space and time and physics—"

"Wait!" Samara interrupted. "You went to MIT?"

"I did indeed," he replied.

"Oh. See, it's just that my brother, Jim, really wants to go there, too," she said. "He's applying this fall to get in for next year. Did you like it?"

"I loved it," Dr. Chance said. His fingers clattered over the computer keyboard. "Perhaps I could write your brother a recommendation. . . ." He hesitated, squinting at the screen. "Well, look at this! My old microscope is making headlines."

Samara, Lily, and I all jerked upright.

"'Break-in at Madison Middle School Prompts Angry Response from Parents,'" he read. He scrolled a little farther. "This was just posted on the *Madison Tribune* an hour or so ago . . . Let's see." He began to read aloud: "'Police refuse to name any suspects, but sources close to the investigation say that students were most likely involved. . . . The school's prized possession, a forty-year-old electron microscope, was damaged during the incident. . . . The microscope hadn't been used until the day of the break-in, when a group of students conducted an experiment after school hours. . . .'"

The blood drained from my face. I wondered if those angry parents included my mom. If they did, I might as well stay up here on this mountaintop—for good.

"Would you like to hear more?" he asked.

"No!" Samara, Lily, and I exclaimed at the same time.

He glanced over his shoulder.

I forced an awkward laugh. "How about you show us the video?" I said, desperate to change the subject.

"Yes, yes, good idea." He turned and typed in a few more commands, and the screen went blank. "Well, as you'll see, it relates to everything you mentioned, Nathan: the

Voynich Manuscript, the Phaistos Disk, extremophiles—even intelligent design. It's all there. That's what I meant about such an extraordinary coincidence. What are the odds? What are the odds that a young man like you might show up at my doorstep and speak my language? For that matter, what are the odds that my old microscope would cause such a big fuss in town?" He chuckled and clicked the mouse, and then angled the computer toward us. "The universe truly does work in mysterious ways, as the old saying goes. Just watch and see."

A picture of Mars appeared on the monitor, rotating against the background of black star-filled space.

"Are we Martians?" a voice asked from the speakers. *"Or are we more?"*

I leaned forward, entranced. For better or worse, I instantly forgot about the trouble back in town.

"Imagine this," the voice rumbled. *"Imagine that billions of years ago, a massive meteor crashed into Mars:* Kaboom!"

A cartoonish meteor hurtled across the screen.

"Imagine, back then, that there was water on the Martian surface, and an atmosphere far thicker than there is now. Imagine that life could thrive there, life in the form of eye-shaped microorganisms—creatures known as extremophiles—creatures that are nearly indestructible."

All at once I realized that Samara was giggling.

Lily tried to shush her, but she was giggling, too. Samara swatted her with a pillow.

I glared at them. At least they weren't frightened or offended anymore. Sure, the graphics were cheesy, but there was no denying it: The extremophiles looked exactly like the eye pattern in Samara's DNA, with the same small pupil at its center. And at least now Samara and Lily had proof that people besides me—professors, even—might believe, just possibly, that we could have stumbled upon proof of something alien, too.

"When the meteor struck, these tiny creatures were blasted into space, carried out into the cosmos on the rocky debris. They drifted in this debris until they were dragged into the gravitational field of another planet . . . Earth! And there they took root and evolved into life as we know it today."

The screen darkened. For I second, I worried that the computer had died.

"But is this luck, or chance, or coincidence?" the voice continued. *"Or is it evidence of the universal mind? Think of these indestructible microorganisms as seeds—seeds shaped like eyes, seeds which over billions of years blossomed into intelligent beings."*

The screen suddenly lit up again, this time with a page

from the Voynich Manuscript and a photograph of the Phaistos Disk. I held my breath.

"Question: Why do the greatest mysteries always hint at the greatest truths? It's no accident that we find images of extremophiles within the Voynich Manuscript and Phaistos Disk, nor that many of their symbols appear to relate to agriculture. The first civilized humans were farmers. Life starts with seeds. These seeds blossom into a common intelligence, an endless cycle of reaping and sowing . . ."

At that moment, Samara started giggling uncontrollably.

Dr. Chance clicked the mouse, shutting down the computer.

"I'm really, really sorry," I tried to explain to him, wishing I could stuff a pair of socks into Samara's mouth. "It's just that we're all—"

"No, please," he said. "No need to apologize. If I were your age, I might laugh myself."

Samara sat up straight, catching her breath. "I'm sorry, too," she said. "I am. I don't mean to make fun of you."

Dr. Chance plunked down in his desk chair. "I didn't think you did. How can laughter ever be wrong, if it isn't meant to hurt? Believe me, I've heard a lot worse."

Lily suddenly stood. "Excuse me, Dr. Chance? It was really nice to meet you, but we should probably get going." She surreptitiously kicked my shin with her foot. "We have to be getting back to town. I bet our parents are worried."

"Oh." I took the cue and stood, too, wobbling on my sore legs. I wasn't exactly in the mood to leave, but I didn't feel like arguing with Lily in front of Dr. Chance.

"You really have a nice home," Samara remarked. She pushed herself off the couch and limped over to the door, opening it wide and filling the room with sunshine. "Thanks for inviting us in."

"Thank *you*," he said. "It truly was a pleasure to meet you."

Lily scooted past Samara out onto the porch. "Bye!" she shouted, scrambling down the stairs. "Have a nice day!"

Samara scurried after her.

The door swung shut.

I felt tugged in two directions. Half of me wanted to bolt. The other half wanted to take Dr. Chance up on his offer of breakfast ham. But it wasn't just my empty stomach talking, of course, nor the desire to hole up here and hide from whatever waited for us back in town. I wasn't sure if I could survive another hour-long bike ride. The couch was comfy. I could sit there for hours and pick his brain. Besides, we never did find out what he knew about the electron microscope, or if it might help us figure out who'd stolen those negatives.

"You'd better run along now," Dr. Chance said quietly. "You don't want to worry your friends."

"I guess you're right," I said. "I wish I could stay."

A bittersweet smile curled on his lips. "Some other time," he said. "Please do come back to visit, Nathan, if you ever get a chance. I'd love to show you my video about alien visitors from Alpha Centauri."

Part Six
Lily Frederick

It wasn't until we'd clambered back onto our bikes and were zipping back down the mountain road that I felt like myself again.

Samara was right: The ride home was much, much easier. I caught a glimpse of Madison rooftops through a gap in the trees, spread out like a giant board game below us. The town looked far away. *Too* far. I pedaled faster, out ahead of the other two, wanting to put as much distance as possible between us and that freakish campground. Even if the police *were* looking for us again, I'd rather hide in town. Anywhere was better than Whispering Oaks.

Dr. Chance needed major mental help. I try never, ever to judge, but how could he say all that stuff about Jesus? It's fine not to believe in God; I know lots of people don't . . . but what he said was terrible! Terrible *and* ridiculous! Jesus was an alien? Even Nathan must have thought Dr. Chance was bonkers. I hoped he did, anyway.

"I'm sorry, you guys," Samara shouted over the wind. "Feel free to call me a dope. That was such a colossal waste of time."

"I wouldn't say colossal," Nathan mumbled, barely loud enough to hear.

I would, I silently chipped in. My knuckles whitened on the handlebars. If only Dr. Willis had been there. He *should* have been there, with his whole entire TV crew. Then he could have responded to all those crazy accusations and proved that he wasn't a liar. He could have shown Dr. Chance who and what Jesus *really* was.

Honestly. I mean, if you noodle on the story of Jesus . . . Here's this poor baby. He's the Son of God. And in a way, he *is* God. (I admit I've never been able to work that part out.) He was born in a freezing stable that probably stank of horse manure, and people spat on him his whole life, and he ended up sacrificing himself to save the entire world. How could *he* have anything to do with little bugs that floated through space?

I wanted to tell that to Dr. Chance. I wanted to tell him that Jesus may have traveled through space and time—if that's what heaven is—but he walked among us, too, which was what Dr. Willis meant when he preached about the Word. He meant that God once suffered so that we'll never have to suffer again. God gave the most precious part of himself—his own family—to us. It's so beautiful it can make you cry. To put it simplest of all: The Word is love. And as Dr. Willis said, Jesus was the Word "made flesh," not made into an extremo-whatever.

I frowned at the pavement rushing in a million tiny sparkles under my wheels. I don't know why I was so wound up. Probably I wanted to convince myself that all these strange eye patterns *weren't* the eyes of God. Or it could be that I was just so tired and thirsty and hungry that I'd stopped thinking straight.

"Hey, you guys?" I called. "Do you mind if we stop at Aunt Esther's? She's probably wondering where I am. Plus, she stocked the house with tons of food because I'm staying over this weekend. And if the police want to talk to any of us again, she won't let them in. I promise."

That I knew for sure. Last night she'd nearly had a conniption, shouting at Detectives Rosen and Gulden to leave me alone—*"What kind of policemen see fit to frighten an innocent thirteen-year-old girl? How dare you? You should be ashamed of yourselves!"*—before slamming the phone down on the hook.

"Yeah, I should probably let my mom know I'm okay," Nathan said. "And to be honest, it's something I'd rather not do in person."

"Me neither," Samara agreed. "Nathan, for once you're making perfect sense."

Aunt Esther's car wasn't parked in the driveway.
Uh-oh.
I ditched the bike on the lawn and hurried around the

house to the back porch, where she kept a key under the mat. There was a note taped to the kitchen door.

Lily: If you find this, please call my cell phone or come to church right away. I'm not angry with you, I promise. But when I woke up this morning and found you missing, I got worried sick. The police called again, looking for you. A reporter called, too. I decided to go see Dr. Willis because he does crisis counseling by appointment on Saturdays. I didn't know who else to turn to. This is a crisis! If you're mixed up in something you shouldn't be, you don't have to hide. Just call me!

Love,
Aunt Esther

My body felt as if it had sprung a leak, the warmth draining out of it. I stared down at my feet as Nathan and Samara appeared around the corner.

"What's wrong?" Samara asked.

I tore off the note and handed it to her, then grabbed the key from under the mat and twisted it in the lock. "I feel terrible. We can take turns using the phone."

Nathan and Samara silently trailed behind me into the

narrow kitchen. None of us bothered to take off our helmets. "Help yourself to anything in the fridge if you want," I mumbled. I grabbed the phone off the wall and punched in Aunt Esther's cell phone number.

Samara hunted through the cabinets for some glasses. She watched me apprehensively, pouring us water from the kitchen sink. Nathan slumped down at the table, burying his helmeted head in the crook of his arm.

The line rang twice, three times. In the middle of the fourth ring it clicked.

"Lily!" Aunt Esther cried. "Thank *goodness*! Are you all right?"

"I'm fine, I'm fine—listen, I'm so sorry." My voice quavered. "I didn't want to make you worried. I honestly thought I'd be back before you woke up—"

"Shhh," she said. "It's all right. I'm not mad. Can you get to church?"

"Sure, of course," I said.

"Good. Because Dr. Willis wants to meet you."

"He does?" In spite of all the guilt and regret, I couldn't help feeling a twinge of delight—followed, of course, by shame. He *was* sort of famous, after all. I'd always wondered what it would be like to talk to him alone. "Um . . . isn't he really busy?"

"Well, this break-in at your school has gotten the police and everyone else in town into a twist, and Dr. Willis wants to get to the bottom of it," she said. "He doesn't think the police and the newspaper reporters are helping much."

I swallowed. "What do you mean?"

"I told him about how rude the police were when they called you last night, and he's just as up in arms as I am over it. But what's really riled him is how the school even let you conduct this experiment in the first place. So he wants to talk to you about it."

Shame quickly turned to worry. "Is he mad?" I asked.

"Oh, no, Lily, not at you. He's mad at your school. And at the police, for the way they're handling the investigation. According to the reporter who called me this morning, this electron microscope is a big deal. Did you know that your school is the only school in the whole country that has one?"

"Yeah, but . . ." I wasn't sure why that was important. Because it was damaged during the theft? Because maybe damaging our microscope was just as bad as damaging, say, a rare work of art? *Please, God, let the microscope be okay.* My thoughts started to race again. If everyone believed that *we* were the thieves, we were in even bigger trouble than I'd imagined. No wonder reporters were curious. No wonder we'd already made headlines in the newspaper. . . .

169

"Lily, listen to me," Aunt Esther said. "Dr. Willis wanted me to tell you that you don't have to talk to those two detectives if you don't want to. You don't have to talk to any reporters, either. You can talk to him first, in church. They aren't allowed inside."

"They aren't?" I knew that people had to have tickets to get into his church on Sunday, but I was pretty sure that it was open to everyone else the rest of the time.

"It's the law," she said firmly. "Dr. Willis calls it 'sanctuary.' I call it Providence."

I swallowed. I'd heard those words before, but neither made any sense. "I'll be right there," I told her. "But, Aunt Esther, is it all right if my two friends come? The police might come looking for them, too."

"Yes, yes, of course. But hurry, okay?"

"I will. Bye." I hung up the phone.

Samara handed me a glass of water. "What was that all about?" she asked.

"Um . . . Dr. Willis wants to talk to me." I took a few sips, my mind whirling. "Well, I guess he wants to talk to all of us, because of the experiment and the break-in. The police are looking for us, but Dr. Willis wants to talk to us first. And we don't have to talk to the police if we're at church."

Nathan lifted his head. "We don't? Why not?"

"It's the law, I guess," I said. "Aunt Esther said it has something to do with sanctuary and Providence. Do you know what that means?"

He nodded. "Yeah, I learned something about that in Hebrew school," he said. "They're both religious words. Sanctuary is, like, a protected place. And Providence means, like, divine intervention."

"Oh." I began to feel better.

Samara finished her water and plunked her glass in the sink. "I hope you're right, Nathan," she said. "Last I heard, Providence was a city in Rhode Island."

After we stuffed ourselves with microwave breakfast burritos and bananas and orange juice, Samara called home. Jim picked up and right away started yelling. I could hear his muffled voice through the phone.

Apparently, Samara's parents hadn't even noticed she was missing until a reporter had called *her* house, too, to ask about the famous microscope. Did Samara know how valuable it was? Was that why she'd stolen the negatives from it?

And as if that weren't bad enough, the police then called and requested that Mr. and Mrs. Brooks come down to the station to answer a few more questions—which they did. They were there then, in fact. Judging from Jim's tone, they hadn't exactly been happy when they'd left the house. They'd instructed Jim to stay put in case Samara turned up.

It was a short conversation. She asked Jim to call their dad to let him know she was okay—and that she'd be right home after a brief pit stop at Church of the Shepherd. Jim asked her if she'd gone insane. (Barked at her, was more like it.) He also told her she was perfectly capable of calling their dad herself. Samara promised she would, but when she hung up, she handed the phone to Nathan.

"I think I'll wait a little bit," she said. "Generally, I can't handle getting bawled out more than twice in one day."

Nathan didn't fare much better. He reached his mom on her cell phone at the police station. She informed him that she was sitting with Samara's parents, Dr. and Mrs. Belle, and Detectives Rosen and Gulden. Everybody was flipping out, and not only because we'd all been missing until then. Nobody could get in touch with Principal Horowitz, either. He'd disappeared, too.

"I hope this means Principal Horowitz did it," Nathan said as he placed the phone back on the hook. "Because if he did, he'd better explain why to my mom."

"To all of our parents," I agreed.

"And to *us*," Samara grumbled.

The three of us trudged outside and picked up our bikes. Even if Principal Horowitz was desperate, I had a hard time believing that he would steal from his own school. Then again, who knew what to believe anymore?

We stood there for a moment on the lawn, wincing at each other as we tightened our helmet straps.

"Well, look on the bright side," Samara said. "If Principal Horowitz is now the prime suspect, maybe the police will leave us alone while they track him down. And we can all just enjoy a nice, normal, pleasant Saturday."

"I sort of have a feeling that a nice, normal, pleasant Saturday isn't in the cards," Nathan said.

"Yeah, you're probably right," she said. "Maybe I'll just hide out at the church until this whole thing blows over. They have bingo games in church basements, right? I could open another casino. Ha! Sorry. Bad joke."

"I know what *I'm* going to do." My jaw tightened. "I'm going to see if Dr. Willis wants to come with me back to Whispering Oaks to set things straight with Dr. Chance."

Samara laughed. "Why? You really want to go back there?"

"Yeah," Nathan said quietly. "What do you have against Dr. Chance, anyway?"

"Are you serious?" I yelled. "He called Dr. Willis a liar! And a criminal! And all kinds of other things!" I shook my head, too flustered to go on. "Dr. Chance needs help. He's completely demented. *And* creepy."

"I don't know," Nathan said. "He just seemed like a sad, lonely old man to me. I felt sorry for him. He practically begged me to come back and visit."

"Hey, then you should tag along with Lily and Dr. Willis," Samara cracked.

I turned away, feeling glum. I hadn't meant to raise my voice or get upset with Nathan. But Dr. Willis *did* deserve to hear what Dr. Chance had said about him. I guess part of me felt that when Dr. Chance had been accusing Dr. Willis of all those things, he'd been accusing me, too. I went to Dr. Willis's church, after all. I believed in the same God he did. Maybe I just wanted Dr. Willis to stand up for *me*.

"I wouldn't mind tagging along," Nathan said after a moment. "He could show me his film clip on Alpha Centauri."

"Alpha what?" Samara asked.

"Alpha Centauri," Nathan repeated. "It's the closest star to our sun. And there's a theory about it. You know how everybody who's seen an alien in real life tells the same story about how they look? How they're always these pale, bug-eyed dwarves?"

Samara gave Nathan a quick once-over. "Go easy on yourself. You're not that short or pale."

"Ha, ha, ha," he said flatly. "No, seriously, there's a reason for that. See, one of the stars in Alpha Centauri is a red dwarf. It's much older than the sun, so its solar rays are dimmer. The aliens there could get away with having big eyes and hairless bodies, because they wouldn't have to protect themselves from solar rays, like we do. And since their sun is so much older than ours, they're probably much more advanced than we are. They're only four light-years away. If they built a spaceship that went nearly the speed of light, they could get to Earth in about eighty years, depending on the physics."

Samara rolled her eyes at me. "You don't say?"

I hoisted my sore right leg over the bike. "Nathan, I really don't want to argue with you anymore. But how about you drop the subject of aliens for a while?"

The mood at Church of the Shepherd is different on a Saturday. You don't sense that same welcoming presence when you open the vestibule doors, something big and invisible and joyous that swallows you right up with hundreds of other people. Without the TV lights, it feels gloomy, like a boarded-up theater. Everything's quiet. Everything echoes.

The empty pews seem to take up too much space, too, as if they don't belong without worshippers to fill them.

"Lily!" Aunt Esther cried. She raced down the aisle and swept me into a hug. "You know, if I weren't so happy to see you, I'd wring your neck," she breathed, nuzzling my ear. "Don't *ever* sneak out like that again."

"I won't," I promised, ashamed.

Aunt Esther pulled away from me and gestured toward the pulpit, where Dr. Willis was studying some papers. "Go on up. He's dying to talk to you."

My pulse quickened. Funny: It was the very first time I'd seen him wearing something other than a suit. He still looked *nice*—with his shock of gray hair and crisp jeans and a dark blazer—only smaller, somehow.

"Aunt Esther, this is my friend Nathan," I said. "And you remember Samara from yesterday, right? She's the one who waited with me after school when I fainted."

Aunt Esther smiled at Samara. "Right." She shook Nathan's hand. "Well, kids, I hope we'll all meet again under better circumstances, huh?"

"Hello, there!" Dr. Willis's voice boomed across the church. He strolled down the steps and waved at the front pew. "I'm glad you made it here safely. Quite a circus out there, what with all the police activity. Please, kids. Come sit down."

I wasn't quite sure what Dr. Willis meant by "quite a circus"—we hadn't seen any police on the way here. On the other hand, we hadn't passed by school, either. Maybe the police were back at the scene of the crime investigating. Or maybe we were just one step ahead of them. Either way, I didn't feel so lucky.

Samara filed into the pew first, followed by Nathan, followed by me.

Dr. Willis graciously shook our hands. He did the double clasp, too: one hand on top of the other, which I liked. I'd done the same thing when I campaigned for class president last spring. People always feel good when you give more than just a regular handshake. Then he gave us all nicknames. "Sammy!" "Nate!" "Lil!" With a chuckle, he eased himself down on the dais steps, facing us. Aunt Esther sat beside him.

"Why the long faces?" he asked us. "You're safe here, you know that?"

I folded my hands in my lap. I wasn't sure what to say.

"I guess I never thought I'd use church as a hideout from the cops," Samara replied after a minute.

"Ha!" he laughed. "Well, consider yourself welcome, Sammy. No police allowed. Unless they've come to pray or ask for forgiveness."

"Okeydokey," she said. "Thanks."

"Yeah, and thanks again for even inviting us in," Nathan added.

"It's the least I can do, Nate," Dr. Willis assured him. "And I want you to know something. If any of you have anything to confess about what happened at school yesterday, it's all right. God forgives you."

"But we didn't do it!" I cried.

He nodded. "I want to believe you, Lil. I want to believe you because I see that you're a good person. It upsets me that your school doesn't do more to protect you."

"What do you mean?" Samara said. "Protect us from what?"

"From false accusations, but more than that, from poisonous ideas," he said sternly. "This so-called fancy microscope at the center of all this madness . . . it has no place in a school like yours. None." Dr. Willis shook his head several times. "It's the devil's looking glass. Wherever it goes, it sows wickedness and confusion. I've seen it destroy lives before. It has a long, sinister history—all of it for evil purposes."

Nathan began to fidget. "Are you, um, talking about Dr. Chance?" he asked.

Dr. Willis's expression darkened. "Do you know him?"

178

"We met him this morning," I blurted out. "And he said all kinds of terrible things about you. He said you're the worst kind of con artist, and that you prey upon the weak . . . and I don't know; I just got so mad!" I took a deep breath. Blood rushed to my face. I stole a quick peek at the saints in the stained-glass windows. I wanted to pray for their help to calm me down, but I realized right then that I had no idea who any of them were. They were strangers—strangers who all looked the same, with bright halos. For the first time ever in church, I suddenly felt very alone.

Dr. Willis leaned forward and laid a hand on my knee. "You don't have to trouble yourself with Dr. Chance," he murmured. "Take pity on him. He's a very lost soul. And I hope Jesus saves him. I surely do."

"But he's not that bad," Nathan protested. "And *he* believes in Jesus. He said so. He just believes a little differently than you do. You can ask him." Nathan lowered his eyes, his tousled bangs hanging in his face.

Dr. Willis fixed him with a grim stare. "He's tricked you, hasn't he?"

"*No,*" Nathan replied. "He just thinks . . . I know it's going to sound crazy . . ."

"Go ahead and speak, son. You have nothing to fear here."

Nathan lifted his head. "See, he's part of this group

that believes in something called the universal mind. It's this theory that Jesus, or God, or whatever you want to call him, exists in a billion different ways on a billion different planets. God spread himself throughout the universe on these tiny microscopic organisms, planting himself everywhere, like seeds. They look like eyes. They look like the pattern we found in Samara's DNA! And *that's* what got all of us so excited yesterday. You can ask our science teacher."

I clenched my fists, my blood boiling again. "Nathan, why don't you tell us what else Dr. Chance believes? That Jesus was an alien who talked to chimps—"

"Shhh, there's no reason to fight," Dr. Willis soothed. "But it's funny you mention chimps, Lil. Because I want to talk to you about bananas."

I blinked at him. *Bananas?*

Dr. Willis stood and began to pace around the dais. "If you want to find God's intelligent design, you don't need that microscope. All you need is a banana."

Samara giggled. I stomped on her foot.

"Why are you laughing, Sammy?" He didn't sound upset, only curious.

"I'm sorry," she said. "It's just . . . I don't know. Bananas are sort of funny. We just ate a bunch for breakfast, actually."

180

His eyes sparkled. "Well, good for you. Bananas are a precious gift from God. Your science teacher would surely agree." He turned to Nathan. "Trust me, Nate."

"Bananas?" Nathan echoed. "Really?"

"That's right," Dr. Willis said. "You see, bananas are healthy, possibly the healthiest food a person can eat. They're chock-full of potassium, the most essential vitamin there is. And think about how easily a banana fits right into your hand, like a telephone. It's a custom grip!"

Why is he talking about bananas? I wondered. I'd hoped for a fiery sermon. I'd hoped to hang on every righteous word like I did on Sundays, or when he broadcast his shows on the radio. He should have been preaching about the Bible's hidden messages, anything to prove Nathan's claptrap wrong. But he didn't sound like himself. He didn't sound all that different from Dr. Chance.

"Think about how easy it is to peel a banana," Dr. Willis continued, his voice lilting. "They come with a built-in tab at the top, like a soda can! And you can toss the peels. They're good for the environment. Milk cartons have an expiration date printed on their tabs, no? Bananas have that expiration date built right into their skins! The colors change, so you know exactly when they're best. Green: not ready; brown: spoiled; yellow:

perfectly ripe . . . What more proof of God's intelligent design do you need?"

I slouched into the pew, deflated.

Nathan sniffed. It echoed through the rafters.

Samara poked my ribs with her elbow. "Dr. Willis, I really want to thank you again for taking us in like this," she said as politely as she could. "But it's not fair of us to ask you to protect us from the police. And besides, we have nothing to hide."

"That's right," Nathan said. He stood. "We didn't vandalize the science lab. We didn't steal the film negatives. And instead of holing up in here, we should be out looking for the person who did it. We shouldn't waste your time."

"Shouldn't you leave the detective work to the police?" Dr. Willis asked.

"But they think *we* did it," Samara said. "And they're probably on their way over here right now, with my parents and Nathan's mom. And *then* what's gonna happen? They'll wait around on the front steps because they're not allowed in—and we'll be stuck in here, not wanting to go out . . . and nothing will be solved. And what's the point of that? Whoever did it is getting off scot-free."

Samara was right. The whole world had gone crazy. It was time for me to stand up and take Samara's lead. It was time for *me* to lead for once. Wasn't that why I'd run for class president? To lead? (Well, actually, if I were going to be completely honest, I ran for class president because Madison Middle School can be a lonely place. I'd always found it hard to get to know people. I figured if I put myself out there and ran for office, people would *have* to get to know me. And I was right. But whatever. I hadn't been elected because I allowed people to yank me in a hundred different directions.) Enough was enough. I marched to the side door. We were going to find those missing negatives *now.* The three of us. By ourselves. Period.

"Lily, where are you going?" Aunt Esther called after me. "Come back!"

"I'll come back as soon as we solve this crime." My throat tightened. I knew if I turned around, I might chicken out. "We have to clear ourselves, okay?"

Samara and Nathan hurried after me. I swung the door shut behind us. I should have thanked Dr. Willis, for the sake of manners, but there was nothing to thank him for. He hadn't tried to save us from anything, as far as I could tell. He'd tried to lecture us about bananas. Worse than that, he hadn't acted like he believed us.

"Where are we going?" Samara whispered.

"School," I said.

"Why are we going *there*?" Nathan squeaked.

"Because school is the best place to hunt for a principal," I told him.

Madison Middle School's front doors were unlocked.

Very strange. Madison Middle School's front doors were *never* unlocked on the weekends. As class president, I knew that for a fact. Then again, I should have come to expect strangeness. As Wendy Melvin might put it, strangeness was the new normal.

We dropped our bikes and helmets on the lawn. I scanned the area for any nosy reporters on a stakeout. My ears perked up, listening for sirens wailing in the distance. Nope. Nobody had bothered to chase after us. Either that or they had already moved on. I wasn't sure if that was good or bad.

"You really think we'll find Principal Horowitz here?" Nathan asked.

"Hey, it couldn't hurt to look," Samara said. "Anyway, criminals always return to the scene of the crime, right?"

"You know, I didn't think about that," I admitted. "I just figured if we poked around his office, we might find a clue as to where he's run off to."

Samara shot me a rueful glance. "I really am a dope," she

said. "We should have come here first thing. My legs feel as if they're about to fall off."

"Mine feel as if they already have," Nathan moaned.

The three of us tiptoed down the long hall toward Principal Horowitz's office.

The mood at school on a Saturday is pretty much the same as at Church of the Shepherd: desolate. It's dark and empty and full of whispering echoes. The whole place feels like a giant warning sign: *NO TRESPASSING. GET OUT.*

"Hey, look," Samara hissed. "Principal Horowitz's door is open."

I swallowed. She was right. A narrow shaft of sunlight sliced from his office across the hallway. My legs shuddered, and not from the bike ride.

Voices drifted toward us, followed by laughter.

His laughter.

My heart skipped a beat. *This is it.* Gathering up whatever courage I could, I rushed forward and threw the door wide open.

"Lily?" he gasped.

"Principal Horowitz?"

Clutched in his arms was a bulky picture frame: the photomontage of his wife that used to hang on the far wall. Seated in the chair facing his desk was Mrs.

Horowitz herself. Both were dressed in grubby jeans and worn T-shirts, the kind of outfit grown-ups wear when they spend the day gardening or scrubbing the house.

It didn't appear as if they were trying to hide from anyone. It didn't appear as if they were packing for an escape, either. Quite the opposite: Principal Horowitz looked as if he were moving back *in*. The old fish tank had returned, quietly bubbling on top of the file cabinet.

"What are you doing here?" he asked.

"I . . ." Good question. The fear melted away, leaving only a sticky unpleasantness, like ice cream spilled on a hot sidewalk.

"What are *you* doing here?" Samara shot right back.

"I guess you could say I'm redecorating." He placed the picture frame on his desk, grinning faintly. "Things are back to normal. *Some* things, at any rate."

One by one, our eyes wandered to Mrs. Horowitz.

"It's Lily Frederick, isn't it?" she said with a smile. "We met at the Spring Carnival last year."

"Oh, yes. Hi. Nice to see you again." My voice cracked.

"These other two are Samara Brooks and Nathan Weiss," Principal Horowitz said. "And I'm hoping that they're here to return the missing film negatives." He raised his eyebrows. "Am I correct?"

"But we thought *you* did it," Nathan said.

His lips flattened. "Why on earth? Whatever gave you that idea?"

Another good question. I'd completely forgotten why we suspected him in the first place.

"Well, you were acting sort of strange yesterday," Samara explained apologetically. "I mean, no offense. Just a little jumpier than usual. And then we found out that the police were looking for you, and . . ."

He turned to his wife, his forehead wrinkling. "The police?" he said. He reached into his pants pocket and yanked out his cell phone. Its light was blinking. "Hmm. I probably shouldn't have turned this off."

"It's just that we've been celebrating," Mrs. Horowitz said. "We didn't want anyone to disturb us."

"Yes, I guess you could say we wanted some alone time," he said. "It's a happy day. I didn't want to be distracted by the unfortunate incident in the science lab."

"Me neither," she said. "It's our anniversary."

They smiled shyly at each other.

Oh, boy. I could feel my cheeks turning red. There was no need for Samara to feel like a dope anymore. No, as far as being a dope went, I took first prize. Bursting in on Principal and Mrs. Horowitz like this made our decision to visit Dr. Chance this morning look like a stroke of genius.

"Well, ah, we'll just be on our way," Samara stammered, backing out the door.

"Hold on a minute, Samara," Principal Horowitz said. "You can't expect me to allow you to just run off. Please tell me why you're here. And I want the whole story. Right now. The truth."

"Well . . . ," Samara began.

"You see . . . ," Nathan said.

Before I could fully form my thoughts, it all came pouring out of my mouth in a jumble. How the police had questioned us. How we'd decided to find the culprit ourselves. How at first we'd suspected Mrs. Belle, but couldn't bring ourselves to believe that she'd do anything so awful. How we'd even biked up a mountain to talk to a crazy old man named Dr. Chance. How we'd planned to ask him how a person might wrestle negatives from an electron microscope—and how we'd ended up watching a video about Martian space bugs instead. But before I could get to the part about Church of the Shepherd, Principal Horowitz chuckled.

"Dr. Chance struck me as slightly odd, too," he said.

My eyes bulged. "You know him?"

"Well, yes," Principal Horowitz said. "I met him yesterday."

"You did?" Samara gasped.

"He dropped by school right after lunch, to chat with Mrs. Belle about the microscope. She'd tracked him down the night before. . . ." Principal Horowitz paused, furrowing his brow again. "Can you three please tell me what's going on here?"

Samara, Nathan, and I gaped at each other. The exact same thought occurred to all three of us at the exact same time.

Dr. Chance lied.

He'd claimed he hadn't thought about the electron microscope in "ages." He'd even pretended not to know that it had found its way to Madison Middle School. And most shocking of all, he'd *been* here.

"Principal Horowitz, do you mind if I borrow your cell phone?" Samara asked.

"I'd appreciate it if you told me what this is all about first," he said.

"I will tell you, I promise," she said. "I just have to call Jim. See, we need a lift back to Whispering Oaks. And we need it right away. It'll all make sense after I make this call."

Part Seven
Samara Brooks

Irony

Before we get to what happened next—

I have a confession to make. I didn't tell the whole truth about what went on between Mr. James and me after English class the second day of school.

Yes, our chat unfolded exactly as I told it. Word for word, right up to the part about how he wanted me to rewrite my funniest-moment-of-vacation essay after I read *Hamlet*. But it didn't end there. Mr. James also asked me to take a crack at his first extra-credit assignment of the year. He thought it might help me get into the habit of using my math brain for something other than math.

The assignment, as he'd scribbled on the board, was: *Can anyone show me what "irony" means? In 200 words or less, describe a situation that could be considered ironic. For instance: "I spend all my spare time doing silly extra-credit work for English, and it's my least favorite class. How ironic!"* ☺*!*

Over the next few periods, my mind wandered down one dead end after another, fruitlessly trolling for some incident that might match Mr. James's goofy example. The best I could dredge up was how Jim made me do his math homework even though he claimed to excel at math. I wasn't sure if that was ironic, though, or just plain dumb.

It wasn't until lunch that a bolt of inspiration struck, care of Nathan Weiss.

Oh, and something else I left out—

Nathan tended to dominate the conversation at my little casino table. Mostly, he wound up talking to himself. Whether that was because everybody wanted to concentrate on their cards or because nobody wanted to contribute to a conversation about aliens, I wasn't sure.

That day Wendy Melvin made the mistake of mentioning that she had just seen a big summer blockbuster sci-fi movie.

It was all Nathan needed to get going. He scoffed that sci-fi movies were a waste of time. They were completely unbelievable. There was no way aliens would attack Earth with ray guns. Besides, movie spaceships were a joke because they didn't obey the laws of physics. And soon enough, after he cracked the code in the medieval manuscript, he would prove to everyone that real aliens *had* visited Earth—and not in any spacecraft Hollywood had dreamed up. He wouldn't waste any time or money at the movies watching stupid, expensive special effects, that was for sure. He had better things to do.

He ended up talking pretty much nonstop until the bell rang.

For some reason, all this stuck in my head, so here's what I wrote:

IRONY
BY SAMARA BROOKS

Isn't it weird how in certain sci-fi movies, evil aliens are always dumber than human beings? Think about it. Aliens are obviously supposed to be more advanced. They build fabulous space-ships that defy all the laws of physics. They travel huge distances to get to Earth.

By comparison, human beings stink at build-ing spaceships in real life. They aren't very safe. They even explode sometimes, which is terrible. They've never been able to get us far-ther than the moon, and even that was forty years ago.

So how can it be that dumb human beings always end up thwarting the evil aliens, if we can barely make it off our own planet? That seems kind of "ironic."

The End

PS: Mr. James, I didn't do a word count, but I'm

pretty sure this is way less than two hundred words. I'm hoping that's a good thing.

The reason I bring this up?

With just a little luck, we'd managed to thwart someone way, way smarter than we were. (Someone practically alien, if you'd asked me that afternoon.) And it didn't even take very long.

At least, that's what I was thinking as Jim veered off onto the highway shoulder and screeched to a stop on the hills outside town, just shy of Whispering Oaks.

Jim's Parting Gift

"Are you guys sure you don't want me to come with you?" Jim asked nervously.

I threw the front passenger door open and hopped out onto the gravel. "Yup. We'll take it from here." I stretched for a minute, my bones creaking. When this was all over, I planned on taking a nice, long, hot bath—and then I planned on sleeping straight through until Monday morning.

Lily and Nathan hopped out after me. The sun beat down on us, high overhead. It felt much hotter than it had earlier. Then again, Jim had blasted the AC the whole ride. He likes to keep Mom's car roughly the same temperature as a meat locker. According to him, cold air keeps drivers alert. I thought it was a recipe for pneumonia, but for once I hadn't complained. By giving us a ride up here, he was sure to get in trouble, too.

Jim lowered the driver's side window. "Can I give you my cell phone, at least?"

"Really?" This was a first. Jim didn't even like me *touching* his cell phone. The gesture probably should have made me think twice about my plan, but I couldn't bring myself to be all that scared of a doddering old man.

"Take it," he said, handing it to me.

"Um . . . okay." I shoved it into my pocket. "Thanks."

"Thanks for *everything*," Lily said.

"Yeah, you really went above and beyond," Nathan said.

Jim drummed his fingers on the steering wheel. "To tell you the truth, I was just looking for an excuse to get out of the house. I didn't feel like answering any more dumb questions from reporters about some crazy plot to destroy Madison Middle School's fabulous electron microscope—or waiting around for Mom and Dad to get home from the police station and start freaking out again." He took a deep breath. "Now look, Samara. If anything funny happens, if Dr. Chance tries to pull some sort of craziness, don't be stupid. Call nine-one-one right away. Okay?"

I nodded.

"I'll be right here." Jim turned the key. The engine puttered to a stop. "If you're not back in half an hour, I'm coming in after you."

"Forty-five minutes," I said.

"Samara!" Jim barked. "I'm serious." He glanced at his watch. "It's nearly three. I'm giving you until three-thirty. I mean it."

I glanced at my own watch. "We'll probably have to jog, but fine. See you in a bit." I shuffled across the highway toward the campground entrance.

Nathan and Lily hurried to catch up.

"Why didn't we want Jim to come with us, again?" Nathan asked quietly.

"Because he shouldn't get mixed up in this any more than he has already," I said. "This is *our* problem. *We're* the ones the police are after."

Lily chewed her lip, her eyes on her plodding sneakers. "Surprising Dr. Chance by marching up and knocking on his door just doesn't seem like the best way to handle this. Do you really think he'll come clean if we confront him? Do you really think he'll give up the negatives?"

"If he even has them?" Nathan added.

Hmm. When they phrased my plan like *that,* it sounded dubious to me, too. But I couldn't think of anything better.

"I really do," I said, even if it wasn't the whole truth. "It's a gamble. And you both have to admit, I'm a pretty good gambler, right?"

A Hero, a Moron, or Both

We didn't reach the meadow until three-fifteen.

Knowing Jim, he'd already decided to come after us. He may be a birdbrain, but in the grand scheme of the universe, he's a better brother than most. Plus, on a more practical note, he has a hard time sitting still.

"So here's the deal, you guys," I whispered. "I want you two to wait right here, at the head of the trail." I fished for Jim's cell phone and handed it to Lily. "I'll talk to Dr. Chance myself. If I'm not out in ten minutes, or if you hear anything suspicious, run back to Jim and call nine-one-one."

Lily and Nathan glared at me.

"What?" I said.

"When did you decide *this*?" Nathan snapped. "That wasn't part of the plan."

"Please don't tell me you're trying to be a hero," Lily begged. She tried to give the cell phone back. "You can't just pull a stunt like this on us now."

I clasped my hands behind my back. "I'm not trying to be a hero."

"I don't think you are," Nathan said. "I think you're trying to be a moron. And you're doing a very good job."

I turned toward the farmhouse. "Nothing's going to happen to me, all right? But the reason I'm doing this is because no matter how you slice it, I'm as guilty as Dr. Chance. I'm the one who conned you into gambling. I'm the one who conned Principal Horowitz into letting us use the microscope. I'm the one who started this insanity, and I'm the one who's going to finish it."

Instead of waiting for them to answer, I whirled and ran as fast as I could, stumbling in the grass—and kept right on running up the porch steps. I pounded on the door and held my breath. My heart thumped inside my chest.

The door creaked open.

Dr. Chance smiled sadly, almost as if he were expecting me.

"Well, well," he said. "I don't suppose you've come back to see my video about Alpha Centauri, have you, Samara Brooks?"

Watching From Afar

"You know my last name?" I asked.

He nodded. "I do."

"How—"

"I'll tell you. I should have told you this morning, but I lost my nerve." He peered over my shoulder across the field. "Don't your friends want to come in?"

"I—I told them to wait," I stammered.

He patted my arm. "I'm glad I have you alone. I have something for you. Rather, I want to return something that's rightfully yours." He propped the door open and disappeared inside. A moment later he puttered back onto the porch and extended a hand. There, in his wizened fingers, was a tiny spool of black plastic.

The air flowed from my lungs. "So it was you," I murmured.

"It was me," he said.

I took the negatives from him. They felt brittle, as if they'd crumble if I made a fist. It didn't make sense. How could *this* have caused so much trouble?

"When I spoke to your science teacher yesterday morning, she told me about your experiment," he confessed. "I thought it was so marvelous that someone so young could be so inventive and curious. It sounded like something I might have done as a child—to show how DNA, our very essence, could prove that we human beings are all the same."

"Then I don't get it," I said. "Why would you want to steal the results?"

"Because your teacher happened to mention the name of this student. She told me her name was Samara Brooks. A name I knew."

I shook my head, my chest tight. "How?"

"It's my daughter's name. A daughter I've been watching from afar."

My Mother's Nose

The porch seemed to melt beneath my feet, sucking me down into the earth and spitting me back up again. The bright afternoon sky turned black as outer space—and I squeezed my eyes shut as tightly as I could, feeling the universe whirl me around and around like a poker chip wheel. When I finally opened them again, Dr. Chance's eyes were glistening back at me.

The words still didn't quite sink in.

My daughter's name.

Me. Samara Brooks.

"I wondered if someday you might try to find me, but I never imagined it would be like this," he said. "That's why I panicked when I heard your name. Knowing how very bright you are, I wondered if you might use those film negatives to match them with your biological father's DNA. I thought you might go searching for me. And I thought it was too soon. I wanted you to wait until you were older. You're only a child. You *have* your parents. It's too much to handle."

A tiny lump began to swell inside my throat. I wanted to tell him that *this* was too much to handle, but the lump prevented the words from getting out.

"Samara, listen to me," he whispered. "The last thing I want to do is hurt you. I know you're wondering why I gave you up. And someday I'll tell you. But for now, I want you to know that it wasn't for lack of love. I made sure you ended up with a family who loves you, too, and can take care of you far better than I could. Always remember that."

I shook my head, unable to process any of his words. I could only think of Jim, and how he'd asked me if I'd staged the experiment just to get my hands on a tool to search for my biological parents.

I hadn't—yet here I was.

The experiment had led me here anyway. No odds could explain it. It was beyond coincidence. It was impossible. I remembered Nathan's e-mail: *He has the same eye pattern in his DNA that you do!*

"There's something else," he said. He hurried back inside and rifled through his desk, then returned with a small plastic thermos. It was the same beige color as the electron microscope. "Put the negatives in there. You'll want to protect them from the sunlight. They're very, very valuable—and not just because they link you to me."

"What do you mean?" I said, my voice thick.

"Your friend Nathan is right," Dr. Chance whispered. His smile was tinged with sadness. "At least, I believe he is. I've spent all day with these negatives, and I can't explain it any better than he can. I believe that this image you've stumbled upon, that I once stumbled upon myself . . . I believe it *is* proof of something bigger and greater than we are. It's like a signature, letting us know it's been there. Or better, it's a stamp of approval, letting us know that we're a part of it, too."

I shook my head, not wanting to hear any more. It *was* bigger than me. All of it: the eye pattern, the wild theories, the science, the religion—the whole mess.

He unscrewed the cap and tilted the thermos toward me.

My trembling fingers seemed to obey him without my wanting them to. The spool of negatives vanished inside. I caught a whiff of chicken soup. My nose wrinkled.

He chuckled softly. "No matter how hard I try to clean it, I can never get rid of the smell," he said, screwing the cap tightly and placing the thermos in my hands. "It's funny. Looking at you now . . . You know something? You have your mother's nose."

A Familiar Cough

"Samara!" Lily and Nathan called.

I jerked and spun around. Both were scrambling toward us across the meadow.

"What is it?"

"The police are here!" Nathan said, gasping.

I held my breath. Sure enough, from deep in the woods, I heard the faint strains of a long, wheezing, hacking cough.

"Go," Dr. Chance whispered. "The police will want to keep these negatives. But they belong to you."

I whirled back to face him. "What are you saying? Won't—"

"The police are my responsibility. I committed a crime and attempted to cover it up. I even made a mess of your science lab so no one would suspect what I was really after." His eyes moistened. "It's shameful, and I need to own up to it. And you deserve the results of your own experiment. They're yours."

My legs froze on the porch. I couldn't move.

"Run around back," he whispered. "The path there will take you around the other side of the summit and lead you back to the campground. Go! Now!"

At that moment, my mind seemed to shut down for good. My body took over, tossing me down the porch steps and hurling me onto the trail on the other side of the house. My fingers wrapped tightly around the thermos. Lily and Nathan dashed after me. We ran silently through the woods—deeper and deeper, swatting branches and leaping over roots. We ran until my lungs were on fire.

Finally, I pulled up short. I hunched forward, my hands on my knees. Lily's and Nathan's faces had both turned bright red. I suppose mine was probably bright red, too.

They looked at me.

"So," Lily managed between gasps. "What did Dr. Chance say, anyway?"

A Swiss Army Knife, a Pencil, and a Notepad

Only later, when I realized we were completely and utterly lost, did I allow myself to cry about what I'd told them.

I cried for a good long time. The tears tasted warm and salty.

Lily and Nathan sat beside me on the forest floor. Lily laid her hand on my shoulder.

"I'm sorry I led you guys off the trail," I murmured.

"It wasn't your fault," Nathan said. "We all got mixed up."

I wiped my cheeks, blinking at the trees. "There seems to be a clearing over there," I said, pointing toward a spot of brightness maybe forty yards away.

"The best thing to do when you're lost is to stay in one place, but we might as well look," Lily said. She reached into her pocket and jabbed at Jim's cell phone, frowning as she brought it to her ear. "Nope. No reception here, either."

"I'll go check out the clearing," Nathan said.

Lily and I hopped up and shambled after him.

We emerged on a tiny precipice overlooking a valley of fields and farmhouses, split by a tiny two-lane road. The sun was still very hot in the sky. Somehow, in all our aimless hiking, we must have found our way over to the other side of the hills. And now we were stuck. All we had was an out-of-range cell phone and a thermos with no water. That, and each other.

"What time is it?" Lily asked.

I peeked at my watch. "Four," I said.

"Maybe we should build a fire before it gets too dark," Nathan said. "The smoke might help people find us."

"How will we do that?" I asked, sniffling.

Nathan pulled a Swiss Army knife from his pocket. Before I could ask what he was doing with a knife, he dropped it on the ground and bent over to clear away some brush. Next, he assembled a tiny circle of rocks around the bare dirt patch. In several jerky motions, he heaped some dry leaves in the center, and then fluffed them as if he were tossing a salad. When he was satisfied, he seized the knife again—

flicking open a tiny magnifying glass and positioning it directly beneath the sun.

Slowly, surely, the leaves began to darken and crackle.

"Grab some twigs!" Nathan shouted.

Lily and I rushed to obey. A minute later, a tiny fire was raging. Incredible. I almost managed to smile as I slumped beside it.

"What other surprises do you have in your pockets?" I asked.

"Yeah, you didn't happen to bring any snacks, did you?" Lily asked hopefully.

Nathan shook his head, staring at the flames. "Just a notepad and a pencil. I always bring a notepad and a pencil with me wherever I go."

"Why's that?" Lily asked.

"Because you never know when you're gonna come across something you might want to write down," he said. "Especially if you're trying to crack a code."

Dear Universal Mind, or Aliens, or God, or Whoever You Are . . .

Once it grew dark—as in, stars-and-moon-in-the-sky dark— I resigned myself to the possibility that we might have to spend the night on this cliff. There were worse things, I supposed. Food would have been nice. Water would have been nice, too. But we had a warm fire. Gazing down at the twinkling lights of the valley, I was certain that someone would eventually spot us up here.

Every now and then, an engine would purr in the far distance. Headlights would appear on the road—winking through the night before disappearing again.

I pictured people snug in their cars, talking and laughing, speeding home to their cozy beds.

I wondered about Jim. I wondered about my parents. My *real* parents, Mom and Dad. I wondered what I would tell them.

"That traffic is annoying," Nathan remarked. "It's so close, but even if we shouted at the top of our lungs, nobody would be able to hear us."

"I like it," Lily said. "It's white noise. It sounds like a stream. Noise like that helps you sleep, did you know that?"

"Mmm," I murmured. "Sleep." I was conning myself, though. There was no way I'd be able to fall asleep tonight.

If Nathan and Lily were at all scared, they didn't show it. Maybe they were as confident as I was that we'd be found soon. Or maybe they were just acting calm for my sake. I'd unloaded so much on them that I wouldn't have been surprised if *they'd* broken down. But they never did. Which was probably why, in spite of everything, I still managed to feel just the slightest bit serene. I wasn't alone.

My eyes drifted down to the thermos, silhouetted against the flames.

For the very first time in my life, I did something I never imagined I'd do. I began a conversation inside my head with somebody or something that wasn't there. I wondered if that was what prayer was. I'd have to ask Lily sometime, when this was all over. It didn't *feel* like a prayer, but then again, I wasn't religious. Aside from today, I'd hardly ever made it to church.

Dear Universal Mind, or Aliens, or God, or whoever you are,

First off: Bravo. I have to hand it to you. I didn't see this one coming.

Maybe Dr. Willis was right—at least about one thing. I don't think Madison Middle School's fabulous electron microscope is the devil's looking glass, but it might have given us a peek at something we weren't supposed to see.

I mean, if you really wanted to show yourself, wouldn't you call out to us with a huge booming voice from the sky?

But no, you probably wouldn't. That's the way we communicate, not you. You don't use words. You use math.

That's what gets me: the math of it. When the math doesn't add up, it must be proof of something. Better proof even than the eye pattern, if that really is your signature.

I got lucky on the losing-est bet I ever made, and lucky in a way I hadn't even admitted to myself. Come on, a cafeteria casino?

Yes, the house always wins. But not like this. I hadn't gambled on finding my biological father. I'd gambled on making "drama," which was just a code word all along for "friends"—and I came up lucky twice.

The odds are just too small for that. As small as what we found in my DNA.

The DNA part of all this is important somehow, isn't it? I'm just not sure how. I'm not even sure what you were trying to tell me. But I'm thinking that maybe, just maybe, it could be that Dr. Chance and Dr. Willis were both right. Because with all their jibber-jabber, they were really arguing about the same thing all along: life. How life is planted all around us, how it grows and spreads, and how it's a part of the whole universe.

My mind won't ever stop reeling. Not until I get a chance to talk to Dr. Chance again, sometime far from now. Not until he's ready to tell me why he gave me up for adoption. Not until I can ask him about my biological mother's nose.

But in the meantime, I have a plan.

I'm going to ask Lily and Nathan to make a pact with me. And it's lucky Nathan happened to bring a pad and pencil, because I want to write it all down—to be sure I get it just right. Or is it more than luck? Is that you again, too, pulling the strings? There are so many coincidences I can't even keep track anymore. Even Dr. Chance's last name says something more than what it is.

So, Universal Mind, or Aliens, or God, or whoever you are . . . If your all-seeing eye is watching, I hope it's winking at me. Or maybe you're just conning me for now, until you're ready to hit me with an even bigger surprise. I'm pretty sure you like to gamble. Am I right?

Wait— Jim's phone is ringing!

I better go. Maybe someday we'll get a chance to count to five together.

Your friend,

Samara Brooks

PS: Thanks.

Epilogue:
What Probably
Wouldn't Have Happened the
Following Monday

All life *is* chance, as they say. But it's funny how what goes on in your life can affect so many other lives. I never really gave much thought to that sort of thing until Nathan, Lily, and I were finally rescued from that mountaintop. (As it turned out, it took everyone another four hours to finally track us down after Jim managed to get through to me. None of us got home until six a.m. on Sunday.) My point? Odds are that Monday would have turned out a lot differently for a lot of people if none of this insanity had ever happened.

For starters, Dr. Chance probably wouldn't be in jail right now. He refuses to talk to anyone or comment until the trial is over.

Detectives Gulden and Rosen probably wouldn't have been promoted to co-chief detectives of the Madison Police Department. Even the mayor made a public statement about how appreciative he was of their swift detective work. School safety is now *the* number one priority. All the angry parents were very happy with this news, mine included.

I probably wouldn't have shut down my mini-casino for

good. (Frankly, I'd rather spend lunch eating with my friends.)

Wendy Melvin and Constantine Romulus probably wouldn't have started a *new* gambling ring, which meets in the schoolyard instead of the cafeteria.

Lily probably wouldn't have resigned as class president. She says she wants more time to spend with her friends, too. Not that being class president really took up all that much time—or so she told Nathan and me at lunch.

Principal Horowitz and Mrs. Belle probably wouldn't have given the electron microscope back to the police department—at least until it's fixed. And I'm betting that Principal Horowitz probably wouldn't have announced that he was going to take a long-overdue vacation with his wife, and that Mr. James would be in charge until he came back.

Nathan Weiss probably wouldn't have given up trying to crack the codes in the Voynich Manuscript and the Phaistos Disk. Like Lily and me, he also says he wants to spend more time with friends. (Plus he wants to spend more time with his mom, cracking the Bible Code, which he thinks might be easier to crack than the other codes, anyway.)

Lily's parents probably wouldn't have felt *nearly* so guilty about running off to Vegas over the weekend. They promise

214

never to go back again—that is, at least until Lily is old enough to go with them.

My parents probably wouldn't have apologized for insisting that I make more of an effort to "fit in." They also probably wouldn't have grounded me until Thanksgiving, either, for disappearing all day Saturday.

Lily's aunt Esther probably wouldn't be looking for a new church.

Dr. Willis . . . well, he probably would have delivered the exact same *Gettin' Gospel* sermon as he'd already planned: "The Devil's Looking Glass: Peeking into Places Where God Doesn't Want You to Peek."

Oh, and finally—Jim probably wouldn't have given up on applying to MIT. He says he wants to move to Vegas and become a blackjack dealer instead. Given everything that happened with Dr. Chance and Madison Middle School's fabulous electron microscope, he also says that becoming a big-shot scientist probably isn't all it's cracked up to be, anyway.

Growing up, author **Daniel Ehrenhaft** often wondered if there was an intelligent alien presence in the universe, and if so, whether it was any good at poker or blackjack. He never placed any bets on proving the existence of gambling aliens, but he did hope to write about them one day in a book. He has written numerous novels for children and young adults, including *The Last Dog on Earth*, *10 Things to Do Before I Die*, and *Tell It to Naomi*. He lives in Brooklyn with his wife, author Jessica Wollman, and two ill-behaved pets.